a healing heart

Riverview Series Book 1

You are Stronger than
you think

Melissa A. Hanson

Melissa Hanson

First Edition ISBN-13: 978-0615600741 / ISBN-10: 0615600743
Second Edition ISBN-13: 978-0-9965485-0-2
Second Edition EPUB: 978-0-9965485-1-9

Cover Layout & Design: Melissa A. Hanson
Front Image: gpointstudio/shutterstock.com
Back Image: sirastock/shutterstock.com

Table of Contents:

Acknowledgments:

A special thanks to all the great babysitters
we've had share our lives.
Each and every one of you has
touched our family.

I'd also like to thank those selected few, who got a preview as I
was writing, giving me the inspiration to keep going,
Thank You!

For Taylor Gustafson Polendo, who had the agony of reading it
one chapter at a time, over months as the story developed.
Your excitement was a great motivator.

and to Jenny Cunvong, who's input throughout
was extremely helpful.

2012 Editing by Kim Godard
2015 Developmental Editing by Erica Orloff

Dedication:

For my husband Eric, the love of my life,
who gave me the inspiration to create this story.

For my two special boys, Cody & Cole

A HEALING HEART

"For it was not into my ear you whispered, but into my heart.
It was not my lips you kissed, but my soul." ~ Judy Garland

PROLOGUE

The atmosphere in the Suburban was light and happy. My family and I were on our way home after a New Year's party, it was late, and I was exhausted. It was a cold night, as it often was in the mountains of northern Oregon, and a light dusting of snow covered the roads. My dad was driving, his right hand linked with my mom's. They still seemed so much in love after seventeen years of marriage.

My younger brother Brandon, who had just turned nine a few days before Christmas, had begged to sit in my usual seat behind my dad, and this time I gave in and let him.

Brooke, my four-year-old sister, was sitting in her car seat behind my mom and, after five minutes, was already fast asleep, holding tightly to her pink satin blanket that she still couldn't be without. I often teased her about it, trying to tell her she was a big girl now, but she loved that thing. I think this was her fourth replacement blanket after the many washings and adventures she had dragged them through.

Climbing into the third row in the Suburban behind my sister, I leaned my head against the back of the seat. My eyes were closed and I was thinking about the fun we'd just had with the Halseys. Getting to stay up late, shooting off firecrackers, and banging on pots and pans never got old. Our family and theirs had been friends forever, and we were always together, going camping, skiing, having BBQs. We were like family.

I'd just dozed off when I heard my parents scream from the front seat and felt the Suburban slide sideways into the oncoming traffic. The sudden impact jolted my siblings awake. A loud sound like a gunshot blasted through the truck as the airbags deployed. My brother's and sister's screams blended with my parents' as tires screeched, glass shattered, and the crunching of metal against metal sliced through the dark night.

My throat burned as I realized I was screaming as well. The Suburban slammed into the guardrail, the impact causing the vehicle to flip. All at once, everything went deathly silent, and I was numb as the truck began to tumble down the left embankment. The rotation made me nauseous as we tumbled over and over.

Shoes, jackets, toys, and sippy cups were tossed throughout the truck. There was a final loud thump, and blackness consumed me.

I was not sure how much time went by before I could hear people talking around me. I was groggy, and my body felt heavy and sore. Trying to open my eyes was near impossible; it was like they were sealed shut. Forcing them open I caught sight of my sister's beloved blanket, lying a few feet from me, splattered with blood. Stunned and frightened, I succumbed to the warm and reassuring darkness that engulfed my mind and fell into a deep sleep.

A HEALING HEART

<u>CHAPTER</u>
ONE

$\mathcal{M}y$ ear-piercing scream woke me, and I bolted straight up in bed. My heart pounded in my chest, and I couldn't get it to slow down. I glanced at the clock next to the bed and realized it was only four a.m. I wasn't surprised that no one had come to see why I'd screamed; it was a common occurrence these days. That night a little over two years before still haunted me. I sometimes wondered if I'd ever sleep through the night again without being tormented. So many times I questioned why I survived when no one else did, why I had escaped with such minor injuries when the rest of my family had been killed.

My parents had been pronounced dead at the scene. Brandon had made it to the hospital, but his internal injuries were just too much for his little body, and he was gone before the sun broke through the clouds the following morning. Brooke had lasted the longest. I actually thought she might pull through, but after a week of improvement, her damaged organs couldn't fight anymore and she slipped away from me as well. I had sat by her bedside holding her hand, wishing for a miracle that never came. Those I loved the most were torn from me, and I was living now with my aunt and uncle in Southern California and a huge hole in my heart.

For the past two years, I had shared a room with my cousin Darcy. Darcy was two years older and had moved to Washington the previous fall to attend college. I'm sure, as much as she loved me, she was happy to get away. Maybe she could find peace sleeping again instead of being woken up almost every night with the nightmares that plagued me.

Tanner, my other cousin, was five years older and was already attending college when I moved into the house. He had been spared most of my night terrors, but during his visits home on vacations, he'd experienced them as well. I hated feeling like such a burden to my aunt and uncle and wished that the nightmares would stop.

My aunt had found a therapist for me to talk to after the accident, but even she was unable to help me chase away the nightmares. Her only advice to me after months of sessions was that time would help, and eventually they should lessen. Two years later, I was beginning to think I would never be free of them.

There was no sense in trying to go back to sleep; once I woke up, I was up. Slipping out of bed, the picture of my family on my nightstand caught my eye. It had been taken that last Christmas when my world was still right. I could see the sparkle in my brother's eyes as he leaned over to tickle Brooke, her dimples as she laughed, my parents so happy and so proud of all of us. I turned away, wondering if the pain would ever fade, then grabbed my slippers and went downstairs.

A HEALING HEART

When I reached the kitchen, I made myself some hot chocolate and then sat down on the family room couch to flip through the channels. Of course, at four a.m., there wasn't anything interesting on, but it was too early to start getting ready for school and I had nothing better to do.

After a couple of hours, I heard my aunt and uncle stirring upstairs, starting to get ready for work. I flipped off the TV and went back upstairs to get ready for school.

I was in my junior year of high school, with spring break a few weeks away and my seventeenth birthday not long after that. Shortly after I had moved in with my aunt and uncle I had become fast friends with two girls in my class. Mia Kinney and Natasha Wakefield had basically grown up together in Riverview and had accepted me immediately. The three of us were almost inseparable.

Mia had invited me to come skiing with her family in Mammoth during spring break, but I just wasn't up for skiing. It still held such bittersweet memories for me. My family had always gone on ski trips—it was one of the activities we all enjoyed. I loved the snow and the cold, but ever since the night of the accident, snow made me anxious. I knew the fear of the snow itself was irrational, that it hadn't caused the accident, but it still made me uneasy.

Stepping into the shower, the hot water cascading over me felt good and helped ease the tension out of my shoulders. When I felt the water cooling, I figured I'd better get out before I used up all the hot water. I grabbed a towel and padded silently across my room to pull clothes out of my closet. The weather was still cool in Riverview, so I grabbed my favorite pair of jeans and a pink sweater. Back in the bathroom I finished drying my long brown hair and applied my makeup, trying to conceal the dark shadows that were so prominent now under my eyes. Today, my eye color appeared bluer. Some days they were more green; it seemed to depend on what color I was wearing or sometimes my mood. The paleness of my skin accented the deep shadows under my eyes. Tanning was not an option for me; if I was in the sun too long, I turned into a red, crispy mess.

I pulled my hair back in a ponytail, grabbed a pair of silver hoop earrings, and went back downstairs for some breakfast. By the time I reached the kitchen, I could smell the coffee that my aunt Rachelle was brewing. She turned as I came into the kitchen and smiled. She was my mom's twin sister, and it was still hard to look at her features, so like my mom's, but not.

"Morning, Bailey. Can I make you anything for breakfast?"

"No, thanks. I'll just have some cereal."

"Okay, help yourself. Do you have any plans tonight?"

I opened the cupboard, grabbed a bowl and spoon, and then rummaged through the pantry for the cereal. "Umm...not sure. Mia and I may go out for coffee or something. We haven't decided yet." I poured the cereal and milk and walked over to the table.

"That sounds like fun. You need to get out more. Your uncle and I are going out for a while tonight. We'll be out late."

That surprised me. My uncle Eli was a CPA, and he was in full swing for tax season. But I nodded and finished eating my breakfast in silence. My aunt poured more coffee in her car mug, grabbed her purse, and was out the door. She worked in an office as an administrative assistant.

"Bye, Bailey, have a good day at school."

"Bye," I quietly replied as I loaded my dirty dishes in the dishwasher. Just as I was shutting the dishwasher, I heard my uncle coming down the stairs at a rapid pace. He was always running late.

"Morning, Bailey, I'm in a hurry. Did Rachelle leave any coffee for me?"

"Yeah, I think you might get at least a small cup." I smiled at him. My aunt loved her coffee, and leaving any in the pot was rare for her.

"Good, I don't think I'd have had time to run through Starbucks this morning! I still don't know why your aunt doesn't make more coffee in the morning," he complained.

I watched him trying to get the last few drops out of the coffeepot, with not much success. Grabbing my car keys and backpack, I went out the door and walked to my white Chevy Cobalt in the driveway.

It was still cold in the mornings, and I could see my breath in the air. It was going to be a clear day, a nice spring day. I opened the door, tossed my stuff on the passenger seat, and slid into the driver's seat. Starting the engine, I locked my seat belt in place, like I always did, and backed quietly out of the driveway. On the way to school, I took in the surrounding scenery. It was a view I enjoyed; the contrast of the palm trees against the snowcapped mountains in the distance was beautiful. There was something to be said for Riverview:

it seemed to be in the center of everything with the mountains, desert, and beaches all so close.

We had lived here when I was younger, yet I only had a few memories of the town. Right after my brother was born, my parents packed us both up and moved to northern Oregon. My dad had gotten a new job, better pay, and away we went. Most of our extended family was in Southern California, but Oregon wasn't too far, and we had gotten to see them all quite a bit over the years.

Pulling into the student parking lot at school, I parked my car, grabbed my backpack, climbed out of the car, and locked it. English was my first class for the day, and I started walking quickly across the parking lot. I was unzipping my backpack to throw my keys in, not paying much attention to the direction I was going, when I walked right into a wall, or what sure felt like a wall. My keys flew out of my hand, landing loudly on the asphalt. Startled, I gasped and looked up at what had stopped my forward motion so suddenly.

Deep blue eyes looked down intently into my face. It wasn't a wall; it was a classmate, Collin McKenna. He gracefully leaned over, grabbing my keys where they had fallen, barely missing his foot. Collin had just moved into the area the past fall and mostly kept to himself. I didn't know much about him because the only person he spent time with was Quinn Wakefield, the brother of my friend Natasha. Rumors about him were in abundance, and most of the girls in the school were after him, but he didn't seem to be much into the social scene.

"You should pay a little more attention to where you're going," he stated as he held my keys out.

A HEALING HEART

"Sorry," I muttered, reaching to retrieve them.

As he placed the keys in my hand, his fingers lightly brushed my upturned palm, and I felt a tingle race up my arm. He abruptly turned around and walked briskly in the opposite direction.

"Lovely," I thought to myself. What a complete idiot I was; I needed to pay more attention to my surroundings. I finished securing the keys in the pocket of my backpack and started toward my English class. Just before I reached it, Mia came running up to me, her shoulder-length blonde hair bouncing. Her brown eyes sparkled with humor.

"Hey, are you okay?" she asked, almost laughing.

"Yeah, why?"

"I saw your little collision with Collin."

"Oh, that; it was nothing. I just wasn't paying attention to where I was going."

"Uh-huh, sure. Whatever you say! Gotta get to U.S. History, I'll see you at lunch!" With that, she turned and walked in the opposite direction as I stepped into my English classroom and took my seat near the back.

The day sped by in a blur, but I was relieved when it was over. After lunch, dark clouds had rolled into the area and a cool breeze had picked up. It smelled like rain was in the air. Most of my friends dreaded the rain, but not me; it reminded me so much of Oregon, and I always welcomed the wet weather. I drove back to my aunt and uncle's house; it still wasn't "home" to me, and I doubted it ever would be. Upstairs in my room, I pulled my books out and sat down at my desk, opening my window to let the cool air drift inside. I was going to get a head start on some of my homework before Mia and Natasha came to pick me up. The three of us were going to a movie tonight and planned on stopping at the downtown coffee shop where a lot of the kids from the high school hung out.

I was propped up against the headboard on my bed, my laptop open as I tried to finish my history paper, my iPod played my favorite study music, but I couldn't seem to focus. The impact with Collin earlier in the day had rattled me. I'd never paid much attention to him before, but something deep in his eyes had shaken me. I kept replaying the entire less-than-a-minute interaction in my head. It was starting to drive me crazy when Mia's text message came through on my cell phone.

be there in 10

I shut my laptop and went to my bathroom to finish getting ready. Grabbing my cell phone off the desk, I left my room and went downstairs to wait for Mia and Natasha to arrive. On the way out, I sent a quick text to my aunt to let her know where I was going for the evening. Mia pulled up in her green Civic, I climbed into the backseat, and we were on our way to the movie theater. A light mist was starting to fall and wet the streets, just as I had thought would happen earlier in the day.

We got to the theater, and watched the comedy that Natasha had picked out. I never really cared what movie we saw; it was just nice to get out. When the movie was over, I had to admit that Natasha had indeed picked out a good one as we all laughed through most of the film. Piling back into Mia's car, we drove into town to the coffee shop.

After getting our coffee and a piece of coffee cake that we were sharing, we found a table outside under the patio cover, where the outdoor heat lamps were toasty and watched the people walk by. Sitting there, sipping my warm drink, I glanced across the street as the auto parts store was closing down for the night. The cashier inside had his back to the front door, but as he turned to lock the door, I realized it was Collin. I wondered how long he had been working there. I'd never really noticed before, and my friends and I came here a lot. With it being dark outside, I was pretty sure he couldn't see me staring. I had never paid much attention to him before, but now, for some strange reason, I felt an urgency to find out more about him.

The next thing I realized was Natasha waving her hands in front of my face. "Hello? Are you listening?" Natasha sat there with a grin on her small heart-shaped face. Her long, curly black hair was tossed casually over her shoulders, while her blue eyes watched me intently.

"Sorry, what was that?" I quickly asked.

"I just asked if you were still baby-sitting tomorrow night," she repeated.

"Yes," I replied, trying to focus back on my friends. "Why? I don't think I'm needed until later in the afternoon. What's up?"

This time it was Mia who chimed in. "We were going to go do some shopping before spring break was here and just wanted you to come with us."

"That's okay, I'll pass this time. I really need to finish my history paper before Monday, and I think I'm baby-sitting on Sunday too." I really wasn't much up for shopping this weekend. Natasha was going with Mia on her trip to Mammoth, and I knew they would be shopping for ski accessories.

Across the street, I noticed the lights flick off, and shortly after, I heard a car start up. The deep rumbling of the exhaust could be heard as it moved from behind the building toward the street. As the white car pulled out, I couldn't quite tell what year it was, but it looked like a Camaro.

My dad had been into cars, watching TV shows and reading magazines about all the sports cars. He was always interested in finding the newest parts that would produce more horsepower. Some of the information had rubbed off on me when I would spend time with him in the garage as he worked on his latest project.

The Camaro turned in front of us, and my eyes caught the startled gaze of Collin as he drove away from town. Our eyes made contact for only a split second, yet it had seemed forever.

"Wait, wasn't that Collin that just drove by?" Mia asked.

"I'm not sure. It kinda looked like him." I tried to keep my voice even and not betray my curiosity.

"You know you're blushing." Natasha added.

"I am not." My voice was defensive, and I didn't even know why. It didn't really matter anyways. Collin probably had no idea who I even was.

"No need to bite our heads off." Mia laughed. "He's really cute."

A HEALING HEART

"Whatever. Anyways, so what are you guys shopping for?" I asked in an attempt to steer the conversation away from me. One question and my two friends were engrossed into a complete discussion about their systematic approach to shopping the following day.

We finished up our drinks, and after hanging out for a while, it was time to go. On the way home, the rain steadily increased and had become a full downpour by the time we arrived at my aunt and uncle's house. Grabbing my jacket, I flung it over my head as I ducked out of the car, ready to run to the front door.

"Thanks, guys! Have fun tomorrow! I'll see you Monday!" I called to them as I slammed the car door shut and bolted as fast as I could to the front porch.

I pulled my keys out, and unlocking the front door, I let myself in as Mia pulled away from the curb, both friends waving as they drove off. The house was dark and quiet, which meant my aunt and uncle were still out for the night.

Shaking out my wet jacket, I slung it over the back of a chair in the kitchen and went upstairs. Reaching my room, I pulled my clothes off and grabbed my comfy flannel sleep pants and matching cotton T-shirt. After washing my face and brushing my teeth, I picked up my iPod and grabbed the book that I was in the middle of reading, hoping it would help me fall asleep.

That night as I tossed and turned through my ever-present nightmare, there was a new twist. This time in my dream, instead of sinking into complete blackness, I was staring into startling blue eyes, and there was a hand held out, trying to pull me out of the darkness.

CHAPTER TWO

Saturday morning dawned clear and sunny. White puffy clouds had replaced the dark ones, and everything was still wet from the downpour during the night. I rolled over in bed, pushing back the covers, and hit the off button on my alarm, surprised that I had actually slept until the alarm went off. Getting out of bed, I walked to the window and opened it to allow the fresh rain scent to blow into the room. I loved that smell, and I stood there for a minute with my eyes closed just enjoying it. Leaving the window open, I turned away and went to get ready for the day. Today I was babysitting little Riley Howard. He was a cute, spunky two-year-old who always kept me on my toes. His mother, Eileen, was my aunt's hairdresser and was a widow. Her husband had been killed almost two years before while overseas in the marines. I had an instant bond with Eileen the first time I met her. The losses we had both suffered at almost the same time gave us a kinship that I had not expected. Riley would never have any memories of his dad. I at least would always carry precious memories of my family, with me in my heart.

Just thinking about Riley made me smile. I was glad the sun was out this morning. Maybe there was still a chance I could take him to his favorite place, the park. I finished getting ready and went downstairs to grab a quick breakfast before driving over to the Howards' house.

After parking in front of their small Victorian house, I got out of my car and went to the front door. As I opened it and went inside, I heard Riley yell from the upstairs, "BAIWEY!" I smiled. That was as close as he could get to my name.

Setting my backpack down, I waited as he carefully maneuvered the stairs. This was a new accomplishment for him. He'd been going up for a while now, but going down had been a bit more difficult. He got to the bottom step and then ran full speed for my arms. I grabbed him and swung him around.

"Hey, Riley."

Eileen appeared at the top of the steps and smiled as she came downstairs. "Morning, Bailey. It's going to be a long day for me; I might not be home until close to seven p.m. Is that going to be okay? I know it's a Saturday night and you probably have plans. I can try to get my neighbor to stay here if you have to leave."

"It's no problem, really. I don't have any plans tonight. It's just Riley and me. We'll be fine," I said as I set Riley back down on his feet and he took off running. "I was thinking of taking him to the park this afternoon if it dried out. Is that okay?"

"Sure, that would be great. Riley will enjoy that," Eileen said as she gathered up her purse and keys.

"Riley, come here and give me a kiss before I leave." she called.

Riley came tearing around the corner He'd picked up a fire truck and had it in his hand as he leaned over to give his mom a big kiss right on the lips. "Bye, Mommy. Wuv you."

"Bye, buddy. You be a good boy for Bailey, okay?"

"Okay."

"All right. Well, have fun today. I'll see you guys tonight. Bye, Bailey, thanks!"

"Bye, Eileen, we'll see you later."

As Eileen left the house, I snagged Riley again in my arms and carried his squirmy little body to the kitchen to feed him breakfast. After eating a banana and some yogurt, we were off on our activities for the day filled with lots of trucks, stuffed animals, and some of his favorite cartoons.

After lunch and his nap, it had dried out enough outside that I figured we could try the park.

"Are you ready for a trip to the park?" I asked him.

"Yeah! Park! Park! I wanna go to the park!" he shrieked.

Laughing, I bundled up his diaper bag, and we went out to my car with his car seat. After buckling him up, I drove the short distance to his favorite park. I pulled up and was surprised at how many other people had ventured outside today. Parking in the small lot, I got him out of the car and we walked toward the play equipment. It didn't take long before Riley was off and running with the other kids there. He was always so social and made friends wherever we were.

There were several benches scattered around the area with good visibility of the play area. I picked a bench out in the bright sun and sat down. There were a couple of other moms sitting together watching the kids play.

A cute little girl with curly, shoulder-length black hair was playing by herself in the sand. Riley wandered right over to her and promptly sat down, startling her. "Hi," he said.

She looked up and seemed to pull back a bit. "Hi," she said, so quietly I wasn't quite sure she'd even said anything.

Riley smiled and started to play with her, chatting away the whole time. Half of what he was saying didn't make sense, but the little girl didn't seem to mind. After a while, she relaxed and even shared some of her sand toys with Riley.

The pain of remembering my little sister Brooke was starting to lessen a little. The initial stab was still there, but it wasn't as incapacitating as it had once been. Brooke had been four, probably about the same age as the little girl that Riley played with. Anytime I saw a little girl so close in coloring and features, it brought back memories. I tried to push them back into the safe haven in my heart. I knew that my family would always live on in my memory and heart, but it was still hard to deal with them being stripped from me. I turned my attention back to Riley as he played and I sat soaking in the warm sun on my face. It was a peaceful day, and I was determined to allow myself to enjoy it.

A HEALING HEART

~ *Collin* ~

Sitting on a blanket in the shade of a big oak tree, I watched my little sister Lacey as she played in the sand. The park was one of her favorite places, and I tried to bring her as much as I could, since I was all that she had left. My dad worked all the time, and my mom had abandoned us before Lacey had even turned two.

She wasn't even "Mom" anymore to me; I thought of her only as "Krista," and our contact with her was a few letters or e-mails she sent throughout the year. I tried not to dwell on it because it never did any good and only caused me to get angry. Lacey was still so little and not having a real mom around was hard on her. There were always babysitters who would help out, but with our family moving around so much, Lacey never got attached to any of them.

The park was pretty full that day with kids playing on the swings and the other play equipment. A few moms chatted together on a bench nearby. Lacey never played with any of the kids, always keeping to herself. Glancing down at my cell phone, I realized that we'd have to leave soon. I had to work that night and needed to get ready.

I was gathering up our things when I saw the same girl that had run right into me the day before at school. I'd seen her around school a few times but had never paid much attention to her. Her long brown hair was down today. A little toddler in front of her was running as fast as his little feet could take him. She sat on a bench in the sun while the little boy ran right toward Lacey.

My protective instinct was on full alert, and I started moving toward Lacey to make sure she was all right. She seemed a bit frightened by the energetic little boy. But as I watched their interchange, I realized that this actually might be a good thing for Lacey. She needed social interaction with other kids, and the little boy didn't seem to be shy.

Realizing that Lacey was okay, my attention shifted to the slim girl sitting on the bench. A bag lay next to her, and a small blue jacket was thrown over her lap. Intent on the little boy and Lacey, her emotions flickered across her face. She seemed happy, but then it looked almost like a shadow of sadness had washed over her features.

Her eyes were a light color, I knew from our contact the day before, but I didn't know for sure if they were green or blue. She was not gorgeous by model standards, but her classic features made her very attractive. Her face was framed nicely by her hair, which had highlights that were noticeable in the sun. She relaxed against the bench and turned her face upward into the sun, closing her eyes just briefly. Racking my brain for any other information I had about her, my mind drew a blank. I'd have to ask my friend Quinn some questions. I was pretty sure that Quinn's younger sister, Natasha, hung out with her.

I sat there watching her on the bench for a few more minutes when she scanned the area and looked right in my direction. It was almost as if an electric current jolted through me as soon as our eyes made contact. She seemed shocked, and immediately her cheeks turned pink. The glance lasted for a few more seconds before she quickly turned away. Smiling, I picked up our belongings and walked toward her.

~ *Bailey* ~

As I sat on the bench with my eyes closed, an image of a boy; tall, dark hair, bright blue eyes flashed in my head: Collin. I was beginning to think that little encounter yesterday rattled my head a bit. Pushing the memory from me, I opened my eyes and looked across the play area. Riley still sat with the little girl, and they seemed to be having fun. I wasn't surprised Riley had made a friend; he always seemed to make at least one friend every time we came here. Looking past the play area, I noticed a dark shadow against a big tree trunk. It was hard to distinguish the features in the shade, but then it hit me like a lightning bolt. Collin! It couldn't be; my mind was playing tricks. I had just thought about him; there was no way he was sitting on the ground just mere feet away, at a park nonetheless. Blinking, I looked harder and realized I wasn't imagining it. Somehow, some way, it was Collin sitting there, and he was looking right at me.

Horrified to have been caught staring, I looked quickly away. A thousand questions ran through my head, the most pressing one being why was he sitting here at the park? Feeling the heat rush to my cheeks, I hated that I blushed so easily. It was a curse for sure. Fumbling with my bag, I tried to find something to occupy my hands. Maybe he hadn't noticed me. I was pretty sure he didn't really know who I was. I blended in at school, never really drawing attention.

The next thing I knew, a shadow cast across me. I hadn't seen him get up; how had he gotten over here so fast? My heart started pounding in my chest. He was even better looking close up when I had a moment to really pay attention. His mouth turned up slightly in a smile as he looked down at me.

"Hi, I'm Collin McKenna. Sorry I was a bit rude yesterday. Can I sit down here?"

"Uh...yeah, sure. Sorry, you startled me. I'm Bailey, Bailey Walsh." I pulled my bag off the bench and set it at my feet as he sat down next to me.

"Bailey, nice to officially meet you. Is that your brother over there?" he asked while pointing to Riley.

"No, just the little boy I babysit. His name is Riley," I answered, trying to organize my thoughts into something logical. I'd have sworn my brain had just melted; I couldn't seem to put a single rational thought together. What the heck was wrong with me? I felt like a tangle of nerves for absolutely no reason! Get it together, Bailey! I quietly told myself.

"Ahh, I see. He's a cute little kid. Looks like he's a handful."

I smiled. "Yes, for sure, but he's great, and I love the little guy."

"He seems to be enjoying playing with Lacey."

"Lacey?"

"The little girl he's playing with, that's Lacey. She's my sister."

Of all the craziness in the world. What were the chances that Riley would befriend Collin McKenna's little sister?! Of course, I didn't even know he had a little sister. "Riley's very friendly. He always finds someone to befriend at the park," I said as I slid a look in his direction, practically drowning in his clear blue eyes. It was hard to look away.

"Do you come here much?" he asked.

"Whenever I can. It's Riley's favorite thing to do besides playing with his trucks. I babysit for him a lot. I've been babysitting him since he was just a few months old. What about you, do you come here a lot?"

"Yes. I try to bring Lacey when I'm not working."

Looking back at Riley and Lacey in the sand, I noticed that Lacey seemed a bit frantic. She was looking toward the tree that Collin had been sitting under, and I could see the panic in her face.

"You might want to let Lacey know you're over here, I think she's looking for you," I said as I pointed in her direction.

"Lacey!" Collin called as he got up from the bench. She turned quickly at the sound of his voice and relief flooded her face.

"Collin! You scared me!" she cried and ran toward him, hugging him around the legs.

"I'm sorry. I was just over here talking to a friend." He picked her up in his arms and sauntered back over to the bench where I was sitting.

Riley, watching his friend disappear, grabbed her sand toys that she had left behind and brought them back to the bench.

"Hey, Wacey, you forgot your toys," Riley said as he reached us.

"Thanks for bringing those here, Riley. That was being a good helper," I praised him as he set the toys on the ground.

"Welcome! Can you come pway again, Wacey?" he asked.

Lacey, still in Collin's arms, peered down at Riley and shyly nodded her head yes and smiled hesitantly.

Collin, smiling, looked back at me. "Well, I guess that means we're going to have to schedule a play date."

"Pwease, Baiwey! Pwease!" Riley pleaded.

"Sure, Riley," I agreed, smiling as I ruffled his hair. I could never tell him no; that little boy had me wrapped around his little finger and he knew it.

Collin set Lacey back down on the ground and pulled out his cell phone. "Here, let me get your number and we can schedule another time to meet. Lacey's really shy, and this is the first person she's ever wanted to play with."

Numbly, I rattled off my number for him. Before I knew it, I had my phone out, adding his number into my contact list as well. What a crazy day! I wondered if I'd wake up any minute now and realize it was only a dream.

"Well, it was great to meet you, Bailey. I'll call or text you later. Very nice to meet you too, Riley." he said as he leaned down to shake little Riley's hand. "We'll get together soon, I promise. Come on, Lacey, let's get your stuff and get going. I've got to get you home so I can go to work."

The two of them gathered up their stuff and walked toward Collin's car, which I had parked right next to and hadn't even paid attention to. Not like I ever expected to see Collin in a park! I watched them leave and waved back to Collin as he waved in our direction. Riley pulling on my sleeve brought me back into focus.

"Do we hafta go?" he asked forlornly.

"No, we can stay a bit longer; you can go play."

With that, he turned and ran back to the slides looking for a new friend to play with. I sat there in complete disbelief. That did not just happen. It was all in my active imagination. But then I looked at the phone still clutched in my hand and knew that Collin's number was in there.

That evening as I was getting ready for bed, I kept going over in my head every little detail of the time in the park. I had finally come to terms that it had happened but figured Collin was just interested in finding someone for Lacey to play with. I felt full of energy that I didn't know how to burn. I'd never felt this restless before. I was probably blowing the whole thing out of proportion and the feelings I had were probably just one-sided. But deep down there was a glimmer of hope and excitement that ran through me. I was going to have to get some more info on him, though, from Natasha. I would call her first thing in the morning.

I grabbed my book and settled into bed to read for a bit when my phone beeped at me. Reaching over to unplug it from the wall so I could see who had texted me, I about dropped the phone on the floor. It was Collin.

Collin: hey bailey, when's the next time u have riley?
Bailey: 2morrow for a few hours
Collin: time?
Bailey: 10-2
Collin: cool i get off at 12 do u want 2 meet at the park?
Bailey: k
Collin: 1?
Bailey: k

Collin: great! c u then
Bailey: k
Collin: good night!
Bailey: nite

It was official; I was never going to get any sleep tonight, and good grief, was "k" the only word in my vocabulary? He probably thought I was an idiot! I needed more info and I couldn't wait until morning. Sending a text to Natasha, I kept my fingers crossed that she had her phone with her and that she was still up.

hey need to talk call me

I didn't have to wait long; luck was on my side. The phone rang, and it was Natasha.

"Hey, Tasha."

"Are you okay? What's going on?"

Quickly I ran through the afternoon's events with her, giving further details when she asked questions. Then I got to what I really needed from her.

"So…what I was wondering is, what all do you know about him? I know he's been to your house to hang out with Quinn."

"I don't know a lot, Bailey, they always keep to themselves. You know how Quinn is, he never wants me around. I do remember him mentioning his little sister. She's a big part of his life. He seems to work a lot, and then when he's not working, he's taking care of her. He comes over every once in a while. One time he brought her with him. She's a cute little thing, very quiet, and clung to Collin most of the time they were here. My mom tried to give her cookies and she could barely take one, she was so shy. They weren't here long, and they left for some appointment."

"Okay, I was hoping for some more background. Guess I'm just going to have to feel it out and see what happens."

"Sorry I couldn't help more, but I'll see if I can get anything out of Quinn. If I do, or hear anything, I'll let you know."

"Thanks! Sorry to bug you so late."

"Hey, no problem, this is exciting! I'm happy for you, Bailey, you deserve something fun and exciting in your life! And Collin's really, really cute!"

I could already feel the blush in my cheeks, and I was glad she wasn't here to see it. I'm sure she'd have teased me.

"I'll keep you posted. Good night!"

"You better! I think you'll have some good dreams tonight!"

Both Natasha and Mia knew about my nightly nightmares. They'd both witnessed the screaming firsthand during the few sleepovers we'd had together.

"Doubtful, but you never know, right?" I said, trying to be hopeful.

"'Kay. Well, get some sleep and call me as soon as you get home tomorrow!"

"All right. I'll talk to you later. Bye."

"Bye."

I plugged my phone back in, grabbing the book I had discarded earlier, and tried to focus on the story I was reading. After a few minutes of reading the same page over and over, I gave up. Setting it back on the table, I turned the lights out. Morning would be here soon, and I needed to figure out how to prepare for the "play date" later tomorrow afternoon. Rolling over so that I could see the moon out my window, I replayed the afternoon in my head, trying to burn the images into my memory. I felt more alive than I had since before the accident.

CHAPTER THREE

~ *Bailey* ~

Riley was so excited when I told him we were going back to the park today and that his new friend Lacey was supposed to be there as well. I had taken more time getting ready this morning but still didn't feel prepared enough. We had arrived a little before one p.m., and I had picked a bench on the opposite side of the park where I could watch for Collin to arrive and not be taken by surprise. Shortly after we got there, Riley was already running around chasing after a little boy about his age. They were going up and down the slide as fast as they could. The park was emptier today, just the little boy that Riley was playing with and one other boy playing on the swings. Their mom was sitting on a bench nearby reading a magazine. She would look up occasionally to shout at one of the boys to "slow it down" or "be careful."

It was approaching one o'clock, and I kept checking my phone. The butterflies in my stomach were getting worse. By one fifteen I was beginning to get nervous. Either he was late or had decided not to come. My heart was starting to sink. I tried to reel it in; it was crazy for me to be so anxious. Riley, who was oblivious to time, just kept playing, while I was sitting on eggshells. It was then that I heard the distinct low rumble of Collin's car. At least I was almost sure it was his car. My eyes scanned the parking lot driveway for the white Camaro, and sure enough, it was pulling in. I took a deep breath, telling myself that I needed to pull it together.

After he parked, Collin helped Lacey out of the Camaro's small backseat. She got out and waited at the front of the car while Collin shut the door. She placed her small hand in his as they walked together toward the playground.

As they got closer, Riley caught sight of Lacey and raced toward her yelling, "Wacey! Wacey! You came!"

Lacey smiled as she ran off with Riley, leaving Collin to walk in my direction by himself. He waved, and I smiled back, pointing to the empty seat next to me.

He reached the bench quickly and sat down. "Hey, sorry I'm late. I got held up at work."

"No problem. It's fine. Riley's always having fun at the park. How was work?"

He laughed. "It was okay, but dealing with people sometimes can be very frustrating. I'm glad you were able to come today."

"Sure, I have to say I was a little surprised that you asked." I peeked carefully to see what his reaction would be to that one, but he didn't miss a beat.

"Why do you say that? The kids seemed to have had a good time yesterday. I thought it would be more fun for Lacey, and I have to be honest that it gave me an opportunity to see you again." He grinned at me, his blue eyes sparkling.

I thought I could get lost in those eyes if I wasn't careful. I had to turn away; I couldn't hold his gaze as it did funny things to my stomach. "Okay. I guess I don't really know what to say to that."

"Ah, honesty. I like that. So is there a special guy in the picture that I should be worried about? No one is going to come around a corner and lose it because you're talking to me, right?"

Almost bursting out in laughter at that one, I sought out his eyes once more. "No, no one. You're in no danger of being attacked on my account. You sure don't beat around the bush, do you?"

"No. What's the point? Life's too short; you have to live every day like it's your last. That's the way I try to live."

I had to agree with him. I, out of all people, knew that too well. Looking away, I could feel the tears welling up in my eyes, but I would not let him see the anguish in them. I had to pull myself together and quick. His fingers lightly cradled my chin as he turned my face back toward him.

"I'm sorry, did I say something wrong? I didn't mean to make you cry."

I was not going to blabber about my entire life history with him, I was determined. But something in those deep eyes melted all my resolve. The tears slipped silently down my cheek. I could feel their warmth, and then they were gently brushed away with his thumb.

"No, it's okay. It isn't anything you said. It's just that I know how short life can be. Do you know anything about my family?" I asked him quietly, trying to keep my voice even.

"No, I can't say that I've heard anything. Why?"

I decided I might as well give him some background. There was no point in hiding what had happened, it was common knowledge anyway. Sitting up, I looked straight into those eyes and found encouragement and strength in them.

"Two years ago I was in Oregon with my family —my dad, mom, younger brother and sister. Brandon was nine, and Brooke was four. It was New Year's Eve; we had been at our friends' house. They had two girls, and one was my age, the other just a couple years younger. Our parents were in one room, and us kids were all in the game room playing for most of the night. We got to stay up that night and watch the ball drop on TV at midnight. Our parents let us go outside, shoot off firecrackers, and bang on pots and pans. It was a lot of fun for us.

"When it was time to go, my family got into our Suburban and headed home. We weren't going very far; we only lived about ten minutes away. My younger brother had begged to sit in my seat. He usually had to sit all the way in the back, but I let him switch places with me. I never did that, but for some reason, that night I did.

"I climbed in the back behind my little sister's seat. My sister had fallen asleep almost before we backed out of the driveway. My brother was watching the TV screen on the back of my dad's seat. It was just like every other trip home except that night we never made it home." My voice broke on the last syllable.

Closing my eyes, I tried to shut out the rest of it, but it wouldn't go away. I doubted it would ever go away. Opening my eyes, I checked to make sure Riley was still okay. He and Lacey were going up and down the slides. I turned to look back at Collin, who was watching me intently.

"And?"

What was I doing? I never talked like this. Opening it all up was only going to make things worse, I was sure. But I had started this. I had to finish. Taking a deep breath, I continued.

"I don't remember everything, mostly what I was told afterwards. A drunk driver had been on the road that night. He was weaving along the two-lane road and was headed straight for us on our side of the road. My parents' scream woke me. My dad tried to swerve in the opposite direction, but the roads were slippery, and he lost control. The Suburban fishtailed and impacted with the oncoming car. We went over the embankment, and the truck flipped over and over. I thought it would never stop. On the last thud, I hit my head hard on the side of the car and was knocked out.

"Apparently, the drunk driver had passed out after the accident. No one knew we were down the embankment for hours. Finally, a car passed by, noticed the wreckage, and called it in.

"My parents were pronounced dead at the scene. Brandon had sustained a lot of internal injuries. He'd broken both legs, had several broken ribs. He made it until morning. I heard the doctors tell my aunt later that if they had gotten him to the hospital quicker, they might've been able to save him.

"They thought Brooke actually might pull through. The doctors had been able to stop her internal bleeding. She had several surgeries, and during one of them, they had removed one of her kidneys. After a week of improvement, she got an infection. It spread so quickly. She'd been through so much, her little body just couldn't fight anymore. Sitting by her side, I would hold her hand. She was so scared, always holding my hand so tightly. I could see the fear in her eyes, all the tubes connected to her, and then in an instant, she was gone.

"It sent me into shock. I had sustained a concussion; my right arm and right leg were broken. The ribs on my right side had taken a beating and were bruised. My aunt and uncle took me home; it took over a week before I came out of the murky darkness that had surrounded me. If it hadn't been for the pain I was in, I would have thought the whole thing was just a nightmare. From the moment I woke up in my own bed, with my aunt sitting next to me and not my mom, I knew deep down inside, nothing would ever be the same again."

There. I'd actually gotten it all out. Collin was silent for several seconds before he looked right into my eyes. "Oh, Bailey, I'm so sorry. I don't even know what to say." He leaned over, wrapped his arms around me, and pulled me to his chest. He settled his chin softly on the top of my head.

It startled me a little, but then it felt so good and so warm to be there in his strong arms. I could smell his cologne on his shirt, and I breathed it in deeply, the intoxicating scent relaxing me just slightly. As much as I would have loved to stay there forever, I pulled back slightly, and he released me.

Trying to smile and pull myself together, I looked back into his eyes. "Yeah, well, I really try not to think about it. I wonder if the pain will ever ease. Sometimes it's worse than others. Like yesterday, when I saw Lacey sitting there in the sand, the pain of losing Brooke was so strong. They have some similar features; Lacey is the same age Brooke was. Those are times when it brings the pain back. I think the hardest part for me is wondering why and how I was the only one to survive."

He looked deep into my eyes; I could feel his intensity all the way down to my toes, warming me inside. "You feel guilty for surviving?"

"Yes."

"Why? I'm pretty sure there is a reason why you made it. A purpose for you."

I shrugged my shoulders. "It's just something that I don't think I'll ever understand."

He pointed toward Riley, drawing my gaze in that direction. "If you hadn't survived, then that little boy over there would never have known you. Isn't that something good?"

I thought about it for a minute. Truthfully, I really had never wondered if there was a reason why I made it. I had always been consumed by my loss, often wishing I could have joined my family; it would have been a lot easier. Living through it was hard, so very hard sometimes. Many of my therapy sessions had been spent trying to get to the bottom of my unreasonable guilt. But I held onto it; in some fashion it was a lingering way to hold onto my family, to keep my connection to them, and it was hard to sever.

"Yes, I guess it is."

"And I never would have gotten to meet you," he said with a big grin on his face.

"Okay, now you're pushing your luck."

"But it made you smile again. You have a great smile, by the way. It lights up your eyes. Are your eyes blue? I could have sworn they looked almost green yesterday."

"They seem to change colors. Depends on what I'm wearing or my mood, maybe the weather too. I've never really figured it out."

"They are intriguing. I like that."

"Okay, my turn."

"Your turn for what?"

"Questions. You now know a big chunk of my background, and I know so little about you."

"What do you want to know?"

I smiled. "I'll start easy. Where did you move from?"

"Sacramento, this time. We move a lot. My dad's in construction, and we tend to move where the jobs are. He also picks up evening work doing whatever he can find. He's rarely home. He says it's to make sure there is enough money to put food on the table."

"What about your mom?" I was almost sorry I asked as I watched pain cross his face. His eyes got a hard edge to them, and then it was gone so quickly I thought I had imagined it until he answered, and his voice was strained

"My mom left us. It's just my dad, Lacey, and me. With my dad working as much as he does I usually am the one to take care of Lacey."

"Oh... I'm so sorry. I had no idea," I managed to stutter. Lovely, just great. I felt like I had just stuck my huge foot right in my mouth.

He smiled, the tightness in his face had slipped away. "It's okay. She's a great kid, and we have a lot of fun together."

We sat there chatting about the kids as they played, and before too long, it was time for me to get Riley home. I wished I could lengthen the afternoon. It was nice to sit and talk with Collin, and it was amazing how at ease I felt with him. Like we had known each other for years. I'd never felt that way with someone before.

"I've got to get Riley back home."

"Already? Time really flies when you're having fun, huh?"

"Yeah, it does." I turned away and found Riley on a swing with Lacey pushing him. "Riley! We've got to get going."

"NO! Pwaying with Wacey!"

I smiled. I knew that was going to be his answer before he even responded. It was going to be difficult to get him back to the car. "Come on. Your mom's going to be home soon, and it's time for your nap. We'll come back again, I promise."

Lacey stopped pushing Riley, and he got out, not happy. His head hung down, his little mouth in a pout. "I wanna stay!"

Collin stepped in this time. "Hey, buddy, we've got to get going anyway. How about another day?"

Riley looked up at Collin, a bit unsure, but I could see him wavering.

"Promise?" he pleaded, then bit his lower lip. I was beginning to think he was right on the verge of a meltdown.

"I promise."

"'Kay." With that, Riley grabbed Lacey's hand, while Collin and I followed them to the parking lot.

"So, I can pick you up at five tonight, and we can go to dinner," Collin stated as we got to the cars.

"Oh, really? Pretty sure of yourself, huh? Not even going to ask me to go?"

Grinning, his eyes piercing into mine, Collin replied, "No, I know you'll say yes."

I had to laugh at that; he was right. I'd been dreading having to say goodbye, and now I knew I'd see him again in just a few short hours.

"Okay, five sounds fine." I gave him my aunt and uncle's address, buckled Riley into his car seat, and drove out of the parking lot, waving to Collin as we pulled out. He smiled in return. The next few hours were going to feel like a lifetime, and I needed to find something to wear!

I stood in front of my closet, tossing one item of clothing after another on the bed. I could find nothing that I wanted to wear tonight, the clock was ticking slowly away, and I was running out of time. Finally, I settled on a green sweater, my favorite pair of jeans, and a pair of boots.

Returning to my bathroom, the mirror was still steamy from the quick shower I had just taken. I wiped it with my towel so that I could see again. Brushing my wet, tangled hair, I started the long process of blow-drying it. I decided to use my flatiron and pulled pieces of my hair back into a small clip, leaving small wisps of bangs in the front. Carefully, I applied my makeup and sprayed my hair in an attempt to keep it in place. I dabbed my favorite perfume at my wrists and neck. After taking one last look in the mirror, I went back to my room and grabbed the jewelry I had laid out. Glancing at my cell phone, I realized it was almost five, and Collin would be here soon. As I was sitting on my bed, pulling on my boots, the doorbell rang. He was early.

My aunt was downstairs, and she answered the door. I had given her a quick update when I got home, and I was glad she didn't hound me with a bunch of questions. She was happy that I was going out and having fun.

I finished tugging on my boots, then grabbed my cell phone and threw it into my purse. As I got to the top of the stairs, I could see Collin was already standing in the entryway talking with my aunt. He was wearing a long-sleeved, blue Henley shirt, with the top buttons open at his throat, and jeans. His hair was slightly spiked with hair gel; he was simply gorgeous. Still in shock that he'd even asked me out, I was nervous and excited at the same time. As I started down the stairs, his eyes turned in my direction, and he smiled.

"You're early," I stated.

"Only a bit. I was talking with your aunt."

My aunt had turned to look at me, and I could see the big grin on her face. I may not have gotten a bunch of questions when I told her I was going out, but

I was pretty sure I was going to be drilled when I got back.

"You two have fun, but not too late, you've got school tomorrow."

Collin stepped back and waited for me to walk out the door. He came up next to me as we walked down the sidewalk to his car. He opened the passenger door and I slid in. As he shut the door, I buckled my seat belt and waited for him to get in. His car was spotless; he must detail it all the time. The smell of his cologne lingered in the car. Breathing in deeply, I savored the scent, light but so masculine. He opened his door and got in, put the key in the ignition, and started the car. The rumble of the exhaust was even louder than I had thought.

"Is Mexican okay?" he asked as he buckled his seat belt.

"Sure, I love Mexican."

"Great, I know this really good place. It's kind of a hole in the wall, so don't be scared, but the food is awesome."

The butterflies that had been fluttering wildly in my stomach were starting to settle down. We drove off with the music from the radio softly in the background.

"So, how do you like Riverview?" I asked. It seemed a safe enough topic.

"It's okay, probably one of the nicer places we've lived. I like that it's so close to so many different areas. Being able to drive an hour and be at the mountains or the beach is a nice plus. What about you? Do you like it here, or did you like Oregon better?"

"I miss Oregon a lot, but I like it here. My family lived here when I was younger, up until my brother was born and then we moved up to Oregon. We came back to visit family and spend vacations down here. There's a lot more to do here for sure. It was hard at first, but I think that was more just trying to adjust to everything that had happened than the place. I think one of my favorite things is the orange blossoms in the spring. The smell is like nothing else, sweet and so clean. So where else have you lived?" I decided it was his turn to answer more questions.

"Utah, Arizona, Texas, several different cities in California. The longest place we lived was Salt Lake City when I was little, up until Lacey was born."

"And where was your favorite?"

"Here."

There was no hesitation in his voice as he glanced over at me and smiled, causing me to promptly blush. I hated that I blushed so easily; it was so embarrassing!

"Okay. So what do you enjoy doing in your free time?" I asked, trying to steer the conversation in another direction.

"Working on cars. I love the sports cars, Camaros, Trans Ams, Mustangs, 'Vettes. I enjoy doing modifications to them to make them faster."

"Well, I guess that explains your car and the fact that it's in pristine condition."

"There's nothing like driving with total control over the car. The feeling as it moves through turns, the power under the hood. Finding new products that are bigger and better than the previous ones. Taking the time to pull things apart and understand how they work. Being able to fix them when they're broken."

Watching him as he drove, I noticed that he was at ease and in total control, so relaxed behind the wheel, the car almost like it was a part of him. I could sense his underlying strength, the need to push boundaries a bit harder, see where his limitations were. After a twenty-minute drive, we ended up in an area I'd never been before. I wasn't sure I would have ever come here by myself. It was indeed a small little hole in the wall, as he'd said.

He parked the car, and I got out before he could come around to get the door. It was nice to be treated as a lady, but sometimes it felt a little awkward. I was perfectly capable of opening a door by myself.

"Are you sure your car is going to be here when we get done?" I asked as I scanned the area.

He chuckled. "Yes, it'll be fine. I come here a lot. I found it one day driving around with a friend. It really is some of the best Mexican food ever, I promise."

Inside, we were seated in a small corner booth opposite each other. The hostess left us with our menus and walked away.

"Anything you get will be good."

I looked around, a little skeptical. "Okay, I'm trusting you on this one." There were only a few people seated around us, and the place was mostly empty. We ordered our drinks, and Collin added the nachos plate as an appetizer. For dinner, I decided on the cheese enchiladas, while Collin selected a combo platter with several different items on it.

Our nachos arrived quickly, a bonus of an uncrowded restaurant. Collin handed over a plate, took one for himself, and began pulling chips loaded with melted cheese, beans, and jalapeños onto his plate. I cautiously took one and tasted it. I was impressed.

"Wow, okay, that was good," I told Collin after eating a couple of chips slathered in creamy cheese.

"Told you," he said with a big grin. "You doubted me?"

"Well...not really. Let's just say I'm surprised."

"Wait until your dinner gets here."

We finished off the nachos—well, Collin mostly finished off the nachos, as I was still battling a nervous stomach. Our dinners arrived, and Collin dug in to his huge plate. I thought there was no way he was going to finish everything. I bit into my enchiladas and was in heaven. They were the best I'd ever had.

"Okay, you're right, this is the best Mexican food ever. Thanks for bringing me."

"Glad you're enjoying it. I don't get over here very often; usually I'm too busy. I have a couple other favorite places I'll have to introduce you to."

My heart raced at the thought of going out with him again. "I won't doubt you again."

We finished dinner and walked back to the car. Collin again opened the door for me, and I got in. After he was behind the wheel, he began driving back toward Riverview. We were taking a different route home. I looked over at Collin, taking in his perfect profile as he drove through the streets. Sensing my glance, he looked over, catching me looking at him, and smiled.

"I have one other place to show you before I take you home. If you have time."

"Sure." I wasn't ready for the evening to be over, and anything that prolonged him taking me back home sounded like a great idea.

We got off the freeway, an exit past Riverview, and Collin drove down a side road that wound through the low hillsides surrounding the town. After a few minutes, we came around a corner, and the valley with all its lights appeared. It was beautiful; I'd never been here before and wondered how, after spending the last two years here, I could have missed this peaceful place. There was a big turnout at the top that Collin pulled into and stopped the car. We got out, walked over to a bench, and sat overlooking the lights.

"This is amazing! I've never been up here before." I turned to him, excited.

"I found it while I was out exploring one night. I tend to do a lot of driving. It helps me relax and gives me time to think."

We sat there in the dark, silent, taking in the views. I was curious about what was going through his head, wondered if he was having a good time, if he'd really take me out again as he'd hinted. I was drawn to him in a way I'd never been drawn to anyone before. It was exciting and frightening at the same time.

The air was cool, a slight breeze stirring the trees nearby. The stars above us were shining bright and clear. It was so peaceful. It was a bit chilly, and I got cold easily. The breeze caused me to shiver, and Collin noticed. Before I realized what he was doing, he had gone back to the car and retrieved his jacket. As he draped it over my shoulders, a jolt of electricity shot through me when his fingers lightly grazed my shoulders, causing me to shiver again.

"Thanks. I didn't realize how chilly it is out here." His cologne clung to the material; it was hard for me to think straight.

"We won't stay long, I wouldn't want you to get sick. I just thought you might like it here."

"I do. This is so cool. Thanks for bringing me."

"You're welcome."

The romantic side of me wanted him to wrap me in his arms, to kiss me, but the practical side of me was trying to keep things in check, trying to slow things down. They were happening so quickly. I took a deep breath; I needed to enjoy this moment, to remember it. The minutes quietly slipped by, and before too long, it was time to head home. As we walked back to the car, I started to pull off his jacket to return it.

"Just keep it on for the ride home, until you get warmed up."

"Thanks. I should have thought to bring my jacket."

"It's okay."

Collin turned back onto the road, weaving his way through the curvy streets back to town. We arrived at the front of my aunt and uncle's house too quickly, and it was time to go inside. Collin got out and walked me to the door. My aunt had left the front porch lights on, and I could see the lights were on in the house. I knew she would be waiting for me when I got inside.

"Well, here you are. I had fun tonight. Thanks for coming with me."

Pulling off his jacket, I handed it back to him. "Thanks for inviting me, I had a great time."

I stood there uncertain as to what to expect. He took the jacket from me and slung it over his arm. Pulling my keys out of my purse, I started to turn to the door to unlock it. His hand reached out so gently and brushed the side of my cheek. I couldn't move, just looked deep into his blue eyes. His gaze made me warm all through my body.

"'Night," he said so gently, almost a whisper.

"Good night. Thanks again."

"I'll see you at school."

He pulled his hand back, turned, and walked back down the sidewalk to his car. I watched him go, and before he could catch me staring, I finished unlocking the door and went inside. After shutting the door, I spun around, looking back through the peephole. Watching him get in his car, he glanced back up at the house and then pulled away from the curb.

"Well, it looks like you had a good time," my aunt said from behind me, startling me so bad that I jumped.

"What? Uh, yeah. We had a nice time." I could feel the warmth spread across my face.

I locked the front door and started for the stairs. "I'm tired, I've got to get to bed for school in the morning."

"It's okay, Bailey. I'm glad you're going out and having a good time. You deserve it. And he is very cute, I must add. It's good to see you smile again. I've missed that."

I walked over to my aunt and gave her a big hug. I was not the only one who had lost loved ones. My aunt had lost her twin sister, and I knew that she had suffered just as I had over the past couple of years.

"Thanks, Aunt Rachelle. I know I don't always let you know how much I love you guys." Her arms tightened around me, and then she let me go.

I hurried up the stairs and down the hall to my room. I tossed my purse on the desk and fell onto the bed, staring at the ceiling in total disbelief. What a crazy couple of days! What an exciting couple of days! As I laid there thinking I needed to text Mia and Tasha, because I knew they would want all the details, I heard my phone beep. I pulled the phone out of my purse assuming it was Mia or Tasha. But the text was from Collin.

sweet dreams; c u 2morrow

I could scarcely press the right keys as I answered back:

thanks! u 2 had a great time

My next text was a group message to Mia and Tasha:

Bailey: I'm back, had an AWESOME time, I'll give u details 2morrow

They both came back almost immediately:

Mia: u better!
Tasha: glad u had fun! :)
Bailey: =)

Getting ready for bed, I slid under my covers, replaying the entire day in my head. I finally drifted off to sleep, and it was the first time since the accident that my sleep was not tormented by nightmares.

~ *Collin* ~

Staring at the phone that I held in my hand, I still couldn't figure out exactly what my feelings were. In just a matter of days, everything was turned upside down, and I wasn't sure that I liked it. I'd organized my world into one of sense and order, and a nagging sensation tormented me that nothing would be the same again.

Bailey had stirred feelings in me that I'd never felt before. I'd had several girlfriends over the past few years, and we'd always gotten along and had fun, but it was never like this. Even my childhood girlfriend, Savannah, whom I had always been close to, had never stirred such emotions.

I had an overwhelming need to protect Bailey, to comfort her, wishing that I could take all her hurt and pain away. I didn't like feeling that my thoughts and emotions were no longer mine to control, but that they were now somehow tied up with Bailey.

I knew she had wanted to ask more about my mom, but I wasn't ready to bring that pain to the surface. I was used to maintaining tight control over my emotions. Lacey was the only one I seemed to be able to let my guard down with. Even my relationship with my dad was guarded.

I thought my life had been difficult. Since mom had left I'd been bitter that Lacey had been cheated out of a mother, but I realized that in so many ways she was still lucky. Even though Dad wasn't around a lot, he was there, and he did love both of us. I was also there making sure that Lacey had everything she needed. Bailey had lost her entire family, and there was nothing that could replace that.

When it had been time to leave the park, I knew that I wasn't ready to let her go yet. A strong desire to spend more time with her burned inside me. I had to see if I could unravel the mysterious pull that she had on me. I liked nothing better than a challenge.

Dinner had been relaxed and fun. Deciding to take her up to the lookout had been a last-minute decision. It was one of my favorite places that I went to a lot, a place where I could think and unwind. Keeping myself from pulling her in my arms had taken every possible restraint. I didn't want to scare her or push her too quickly. I could be patient and give her some time.

Spring break was coming up in one short week. I wondered if she was going to be gone, or if she was going to stay around town for the two weeks off of school. Secretly, I wished that she'd be home with few plans; it would give me a chance to spend more time with her.

Walking her to the front door, I had longed to kiss her, to know what her lips tasted like. Her eyes had seemed greener tonight, intense, focused. When I touched her cheek, a shot of electricity burned through my arm, which shook me a bit. The chemistry that was beginning to simmer between us baffled me. Girls did not have this effect on me; it was always the other way around. Having the tables turned didn't sit well. I was surprised that saying goodnight had even been vocal and was glad it didn't betray my feeling of being out of control.

Tomorrow was another day, and I wondered what it might bring. Moving from town to town had been hard on Lacey and me, but for the first time, I was happy for this move because it had brought me to Bailey.

CHAPTER FOUR

~ *Bailey* ~

The next morning I overslept my alarm. I couldn't even remember the last time that had happened, and in some ways it felt really good. Now, though, I was in a rush to make it to school on time. Hurrying down the stairs, I reached the kitchen as my aunt was pouring her coffee.

"Morning. Want a cup?"

"No, thanks, I'm running late. I'll just grab a banana. I'll see you later!" I grabbed the banana, my backpack, and keys and was out the door.

"Have a good day!"

"You too."

Getting to school with just a few minutes to spare, I had to sprint across the parking lot to get to my first class on time. I slid into my seat just before the bell rang and tried to focus on our English journal assignment. English was one of my favorite subjects, and our journal assignments were always easy for me to finish. Our topic for the day was to write about a significant event in our life and to explain what impact it had on us currently. Amazingly, the first thought that flashed through my head was not the horrific accident two years ago, but an image of Collin. I could feel the heat already surfacing in my cheeks. Quickly, I tried to push the thought aside and figure out what I was going to write about for the assignment.

Halfway through our journal session, I still had nothing down on paper. I knew I had to get something written to turn in. Finally, I decided to write about the accident, and was surprised when I was done that the raw pain had dulled. My emotions were not a mess like they usually were when I relived that horrible night.

Class ended, I turned in my assignment, and I walked out of the classroom. I was extremely surprised to find Collin leaning casually against the wall just outside the door. His black, snug sweater showed off his broad shoulders. Excitement coursed through my body. Collin looked up just as I reached him.

"Hey, what are you doing here? I didn't realize you had class right after me."

He smiled warmly, "I don't; thought I'd meet you. This is the only class I knew for sure that you had, so I figured I'd walk you to your next class. What class do you have next?"

"Physics. Not particularly one of my favorites, but the teacher is okay; he makes it easier to understand."

Collin fell into step next to me, and we started walking. "What's your next class? I hope it's not across campus. If it is, there's no way you'll make it in time." I was still in a bit of shock that he had searched me out this morning.

"It's okay, I have Government, which is pretty close to the Math building. I'll be fine."

The crisp morning air cut through my lightweight jacket, but I didn't even feel the cold. We went through our schedules comparing classes and teachers, realizing we had a couple of the same teachers. Much too quickly, I realized I was standing in front of the door for my Physics class.

"How about lunch?" he asked.

"Sure. Where do you want to meet?"

"I'll wait for you over by the Shop building. You can bring your friends if you'd like."

"Okay, I'll ask them. I'll see you then." I turned and walked into class and found my seat at the back next to Mia. I had barely sat down before I was getting hit with questions.

"Was that Collin I just saw at the door with you?"

I couldn't keep the smile from my face. "Yeah."

"Wow, that's so cool! Dinner, and now he's walking you to class. That's a big difference from Friday when you about plowed him over."

"I know. It's really weird, I don't even know how to describe it. I feel comfortable with him, like I've known him forever. Can't say as I'm relaxed though; I feel like a constant bundle of nerves around him. I still can't put my finger on it. Everything is so new, so different. Does that make any sense?"

"I guess. I think it's cool. It's fun to see a sparkle in your eye. The dark shadows under your eyes are lighter today too."

"I actually slept pretty good last night, better than I have in a long time."

Before Mia could respond, the teacher launched into our lesson for the day, gravity and acceleration. I tried to focus on the different formulas and examples. I hoped that my next two classes would speed by, but feared that the next couple of hours were going to drag on. Lunch could not come fast enough for me.

Both Mia and Natasha decided to join us for lunch. I knew they wouldn't miss the chance. We walked together toward the Shop building. Collin was already there, waiting for us.

"Collin, these are my best friends, Mia, and you probably already know Natasha."

"Hi, Mia, nice to meet you. Natasha, good to see you again. Are you guys ready to go?"

"Absolutely," Mia chimed in.

Collin motioned us forward and came up on my left side to walk next to me. I could just barely feel the light touch of his hand on the small of my back as we walked toward his car. Mia and Natasha were throwing out options for lunch. In the end, we settled on a burger joint a few blocks from the school. It had some of the best burgers around.

We reached Collin's car, and Mia and Natasha climbed in the cramped backseat. I moved the passenger seat up a bit to try to give them more room.

"I'd say that's almost not even an actual seat." I shot a smile back to them while buckling my seat belt.

A HEALING HEART

"Thank goodness we're not going far. Who can sit back here anyways?" Mia asked.

Collin chuckled, "It's a way for the auto company to call it a four-seat vehicle so that the insurance rates aren't so high."

"Figures," Natasha added. "Still a cool car though, Collin, even with no room back here."

Collin started the car, and we moved slowly through the traffic jam of cars leaving campus for lunch.

"Glad you guys could join us for lunch. I'm a lucky guy to be taking three cute girls out."

Mia, always the confident one responded, "Yes, you are."

By the time we parked, the place was already packed. We placed our order, and Collin paid for our lunch. Mia and Natasha were both impressed and were giving me thumbs-ups when he wasn't looking. Collin caught the flush in my face and, of course, had to comment on it, which made it worse. I wanted to die on the spot. I would get them both back later.

We found a corner booth and sat down. Collin waited until we were all seated before he slid in next to me, his arm brushing mine, just enough for my hair to stand on end and the goose bumps to shiver across me.

"Are you cold?" he asked.

"No, I'm fine," I lied. There was no way I was going to confess what the real issue was.

While waiting for our food to arrive, the conversation was light and casual, and within minutes Collin had totally charmed my friends. He had a good sense of humor and was easygoing.

Lunch slipped by quickly, much too fast for my liking, and we were on our way back to campus. Collin parked, and we climbed out. I had to practically pull Natasha out of her seat behind me while she giggled the entire time. Her laughter was contagious, and she soon had me giggling, making the process to extract her even harder.

"Thanks for lunch, Collin."

"You're welcome, Natasha."

"Yeah, thanks," Mia added

"Thanks for taking us. I guess I'll see you around later?" I questioned.

"I've got work this afternoon, but I'll call you later, if that's okay."

"Yes." Smiling, I turned and walked toward P.E. class with my friends. Looking back over my shoulder after walking a bit, I could see Collin still watching me. I waved, and he nodded his head slightly in acknowledgment.

"Damn, girl, you are luuuucky!"

"Yeah, I'd say. Not only is he cute, but he's fun, and a gentleman to boot. Geez, you never find guys like that," Mia complained.

"It's only been a couple of days, guys. Who knows if he's really interested or just having fun right now."

Mia and Natasha exchanged looks and then pulled me to a stop in front of them.

"Are you blind?" Natasha demanded.

Mia responded like I wasn't even standing there, "She's blind. There is no other logical explanation."

"What are you guys talking about?" I asked.

A HEALING HEART

"Good grief, Bailey, any sane person can see how he looks at you. He's totally wrapped up in you right now, head over heels." Mia's brown eyes were serious. Today she had her blonde hair loose around her face and she kept trying to push her bangs out of her eyes.

"Come on, there's no way... Really? Do you think so?"

"Yes. For sure!" Natasha added.

This gave me a small ray of hope; just maybe, the feelings and emotions that were stirring inside me were mutual. The thought was exhilarating. "Come on, guys, we better hurry, or we're going to be late!"

The week passed almost in a blur. Collin would meet me in the morning at school and take us girls to lunch. After school I would babysit Riley, and Collin had work. The couple of days he didn't work, he would bring Lacey and meet Riley and me at the park. Lacey and Riley were becoming best buddies, and it was fun to watch them interact with each other. In the evenings, he would either call me, or we would spend the night texting while trying to study for our classes. The biggest change of all for me was that I had a week of no nightmares. The dark shadows under my eyes vanished. My aunt and Riley's mom both had commented on it.

Spring break had officially begun. It was Friday night, and Mia and Natasha were packing to go on their trip to Mammoth. They would be gone most of the first week of our two weeks off of school. They would be back for the second week. I walked over to my window and opened it to let in the cool night air. The sweet smell of orange blossoms from a nearby grove wafted in with the breeze. The moon was bright tonight, lighting up the front yard and street. The deep rumble of a car turning the corner brought a smile to my face. I was pretty sure it was Collin; we were headed out to a movie. Surprisingly, he had chosen a romantic comedy instead of the newest thriller that had just been released. The white Camaro turned down our street, and I left my room to meet him.

Downstairs, my aunt and uncle were sprawled out on the couch watching a movie with their big bowl of popcorn between them. Saying goodnight, I walked to the front door just as the doorbell rang. Opening the door, Collin stood waiting for me with a beautiful bouquet of purple tulips in his hands.

"Oh, how pretty! I love tulips!"

"Wow, you look stunning tonight."

"Thank you." I had chosen a jean mini skirt tonight, with a black long-sleeved shirt and a pair of black flats. Spending a little extra time getting ready, I had curled my hair and pinned back my bangs so that they'd stay out of my eyes.

"Come in. I want to put these in water before we leave. You can meet my uncle too." I grinned at Collin's look of slight discomfort.

"Sure."

Entering the kitchen, my tulips immediately caught my aunt's eye, and she was up in a flash to inspect them and help me find a vase.

A HEALING HEART

"These are beautiful. You know that tulips are Bailey's favorite, right?"

"Really? I let Lacey help with the selection. Although I have to admit that her favorite color is purple, so that probably influenced her."

"Uncle Eli, this is Collin McKenna. Collin, Eli Corbit, and you met my aunt Rachelle the other day."

My uncle got up from the couch, and stepped over to the kitchen to shake hands with Collin.

"Hi, Collin, nice to meet you. You take good care of my niece; she's very special to us."

"Yes, sir. I will."

After placing the flowers in the glass vase my aunt had pulled out of the cabinet, I was ready to leave. "Okay, let's get going so we're not late."

"Nice to meet you, Mr. Corbit. Good to see you again, Mrs. Corbit."

"Please just call us Eli and Rachelle. Have fun tonight," my aunt responded.

We walked out to the car and were off to the theater downtown. Once in the car, Collin turned down the radio so I could actually hear him talk.

"So tulips are really your favorite flower?"

Looking at his strong profile made my stomach flutter. "Yeah. They are so simple, yet so elegant. I love all flowers, so if you ever feel the desire to give me flowers again, don't think I'll only enjoy tulips."

His eyes turned in my direction. "Ah, I can take a hint when it's given. Haven't you gotten lots of flowers from special admirers?"

"Umm...no. Those are the first ones I've ever gotten from someone not related to me."

"Are you serious? You've never gotten any type of flowers? No single rose, nothing?"

"Nope. I told you, no one's ever really asked me out before. I've just had friends where we've all gone out as a group."

"I guess I'm just still surprised. I have to say, though, I'm happy to have been the first."

Arriving at the packed theater, Collin parked the car after circling through the parking lot several times, and we walked toward the ticket booth. By the time we found our seats, we had a big bucket of popcorn, drinks, and my favorite movie food, a box of Red Vines. Choosing seats up at the top of the theater, we moved into the middle of the aisle. The lights went down just as we were sitting in our seats, and the previews started.

Collin had the popcorn propped up on his left knee so that it was between us. He had left the armrest up, and my right shoulder would brush his when I would reach into the bucket. The times when our hands made contact left my arm tingling. Halfway through the movie, we had almost completely devoured the popcorn and the Red Vines.

I tried to follow the movie on the screen, but Collin's close proximity made it hard to focus. My hands were folded in my lap when I felt Collin's left hand casually pull my right hand into his, linking his fingers with mine. A shiver moved across my body. I cringed, hoping that Collin wouldn't notice. My heart was pounding. I wondered if he could hear it or feel it beating as the blood was coursing through my hand. He seemed calm, and completely in control, while I felt like I was about to shatter in a million pieces.

The movie ended, and I was surprised but thrilled that Collin didn't let my hand drop from his. Instead, he led me out of the theater with our fingers intertwined. Walking back to his car, we talked about the movie and the things we enjoyed, thought were funny, and found interesting. It was only when he opened the door for me that he let go of my hand. He walked around and got in the driver's side. After starting the car, his hand searched for mine, and he pulled it over to lay on the console between us. I was secretly glad his car wasn't a stick. As we drove through the streets headed to the edge of town, I was pretty sure he was driving to the lookout where he had taken me last week.

When we arrived at the lookout, I was glad there was no one else there. Collin stopped the car, reached in his backseat, and pulled out his jacket.

"Will you be too cold if we sit out there? Or would you rather stay in the car? You can have my jacket if you'd like."

"I'll be okay with your jacket. The view outside with the lights and stars is so much better." Taking his jacket as he handed it over, I put it on.

We sat down on the bench. I leaned against the back and stared at the dark, sparkling sky above, wondering if I might be lucky and catch a glimmer of a falling star.

"What are you looking at?"

"Looking for a falling star."

"So, what are you going to wish for if you do find one?"

"Umm...I'm not sure yet, but I'll come up with something."

He laughed, "I'm sure you will."

There were crickets chirping nearby, and the breeze rustled the leaves in the trees. It was so peaceful, relaxing, or would have been relaxing if the electricity wasn't flowing through my veins. I was excited and felt alive; anticipation of what might come next was keeping me on pins and needles.

His jacket was big, the arms extending well past my hands. I had tried to push the sleeves up, but it was useless; they just fell back down.

"Look! Did you see that?" I had found my falling star, so I quickly closed my eyes and made my wish. When I opened my eyes, I was staring right into the deep, tranquil blue of Collin's.

"No, guess I missed that one. So, what did you wish for?"

"I can't tell you or it won't come true. Don't you know any of the rules?" I teased him.

"Can't say I've ever had a class on the proper protocol for what you are and aren't supposed to do with falling stars."

"Well, then, I guess I'll let you off the hook. But I still can't tell you."

"What if I guess?"

"Nope, still no good."

Our faces had moved closer together, and then Collin's fingers lightly touched my cheeks, so gently. I could feel him pulling me closer. Instinctively, my eyes closed and his lips softly touched mine. My hands found their way to his chest, the beating of his heart noticeable under my right palm. Feeling like fireworks were going off above us, I was almost out of breath like I'd run miles when he pulled back. His hands still holding my face between them, he leaned his forehead against mine, our noses just touching.

"Did I guess right?" His voice was husky, almost at a whisper. I could feel the warmth from his breath.

"Huh?" My brain was not thinking clearly. This was my very first real kiss, and I wanted to imprint the entire thing on my memory so I'd never forget.

"Your wish. Did I guess right?"

"Oh, that. Um, maybe."

Chuckling, "I'll take that as a yes."

Pulling back, he wrapped his arms around me, turning slightly so we were now sitting sideways on the bench, my back leaning against his chest, his head resting on the top of mine, his arms around me, his fingers laced with mine.

"Hmm...this feels just right."

I simply sighed in agreement. Yes, it did feel right, absolutely perfect. Then a shudder of fear slithered up my spine, and I wondered, could I really be so lucky to have found someone so special? Pushing those thoughts away, I was going to enjoy the moment, and for now that was enough.

CHAPTER
FIVE

~ *Bailey* ~

Rolling out of bed, I turned my alarm off. I was looking forward to spending the day at Disneyland. Eileen had been planning to take Riley for a while now and asked if I would go with them. Riley's excitement as he saw everything for the first time would make today a very special day for him. Because of his constant chatter about Lacey after the play dates at the park, Eileen had also invited Collin and Lacey. That would make today even more exciting for me. Collin had to take care of a few things at work this morning, so they would be meeting us there.

The weather was forecast to be sunny and warm, but I knew it would probably get cooler later, so I grabbed a sweatshirt on the way out the door. Driving the short distance to the Howards' house, it was hard for me to keep my excitement down. I parked on the street and was walking up the front steps when I heard Riley's scream of delight inside.

"Mom! It's Baiwey!"

The front door opened before I could even turn the knob. I didn't even have a chance to put my backpack aside when my arms were full of a squirmy little boy.

"Hey, buddy! Are you excited to see Mickey?"

"Yes! And Pwuto, and Goofy!"

Eileen came around the corner with her arms full of clothes. "I'm not sure he even slept last night, he was so wound up. I've just got a few more things to pull together, and we'll be ready to leave."

"Okay, is there anything you need me to do?"

"Riley's only eaten part of his breakfast; maybe you can get him to finish it."

"Sure. Come on, Riley; let's go finish your food. You want to have lots of energy so you can go on all the fun rides."

Riley played with his pancakes but did manage to eat a few more bites. I cleaned up his dishes and washed the syrup from his fingers and face while he wiggled and squealed. Soon after, we were on our way out to Eileen's car, and we were Disneyland bound.

Though it wasn't that far, the trip was long for Riley. He continued to ask the same question over and over: "Are we there yet?" Eileen, who had gotten some background on Collin from my aunt, was of course trying to get as much information from me as she could, asking several questions.

I had been to Disneyland a lot as a kid but had not been back since the summer before the accident. We had come down for our yearly summer vacation, and it had been Brooke's first visit. She had been so thrilled to see her favorite princess, Belle. I was hoping that today's trip wouldn't bring back too many painful memories.

"Is Collin going to call you when they get there?"

"Yes, he thought they might be a couple hours behind us. He was going to try to get done faster, but he wasn't sure when they'd let him go from work."

"Having Lacey there will be even more fun for Riley. Those two have really bonded, haven't they? The days you meet up at the park, that's all I hear about, then the days you don't go to the park, all I hear all day is 'Can we go see Lacey, Mom, please!'"

"Wacey's coming right, Mom?" Riley's little voice traveled from the back seat.

"Yes, sweetie. We'll meet them there."

"Wacey's coming, Baiwey."

"Yes, I know, that's exciting. Eileen, I just wanted to say thanks for inviting Collin and Lacey."

Eileen glanced sideways to look at me, smiling. "It's no problem, Bailey, really. I think it'll be fun. I'm also looking forward to meeting this guy who seems to have come in and swept you off your feet and to finally meet Lacey, who seems to have stolen little Riley's affections."

"Yeah, they really are cute together."

The rest of the drive passed mostly in silence, with just the music from the stereo punctuated by Riley's ever-present "Are we there yet?" mixed in with "Where are we now?"

Before long, we were driving into the massive concrete parking garage. We parked up on the Mickey Mouse level, to Riley's delight. After unloading the stroller and our bags, we loaded Riley up and took the elevator to the ground level so that we could catch the next tram to the main gate. Waiting for the tram, my phone buzzed. It was Collin.

> **Collin:** got out early! on my way to pick up Lacey, will c u soon
> **Bailey:** cool! we're just getting on the tram. can't wait til u get here! :)
> **Collin:** I'll text u when we get there
> **Bailey:** K

"Collin?"

"Yes, he just got finished with work. He's on his way to pick up Lacey and will text me when they get here."

"Wow, that was fast. They won't be far behind us then."

Our tram arrived, and we stepped in. I helped Riley into the center of the long bench seat while Eileen pulled the stroller up and tried to get settled with the bags. It was no wonder that she'd wanted some help on Riley's first trip to the Happiest Place on Earth. Keeping track of a two-year-old with all the stuff needed for him could be a daunting task for one person.

Once inside the park, we walked down Main Street toward Sleeping Beauty Castle; our first stop for the day would be in Fantasyland. Riley had climbed into his stroller, which allowed us to move more quickly through the already packed street. Dumbo was our first ride, and from there, we moved on to Peter Pan, Mr. Toad's Wild Ride, and the King Arthur Carrousel. We had decided to skip Snow White and Pinocchio; we weren't sure if they would scare Riley. Waiting in line for Casey Jr. Circus Train, Collin's text arrived letting us know they were here.

> **Bailey:** we're in fantasyland, in line for Casey Jr then to the tea cups

Collin: k, we'll meet u there

"They're walking in. We'll meet them at the tea cups."

"Perfect. They made pretty good time coming down here."

It was finally our turn, and we climbed in the Monkeys cage. Eileen and I both laughed; how appropriate for little Riley. As the train traveled through Storybook Land, the tiny castles fascinated Riley, and he had his face pushed tightly against the bars. Much too quickly for Riley, the ride was over and we walked toward the tea cups. Parking the stroller along the edge, I scanned the crowds for Collin and Lacey.

"Bailey, I'm going to run Riley to the restroom around the corner while we wait for them to get here."

"Okay." I pulled the bag of Riley's things out from under the stroller and handed it to Eileen.

"Thanks, we'll be right back."

I was leaning against the stroller looking toward the Carrousel when I felt a pair of arms from behind wrap around my waist. I was so startled, a small scream escaped my lips. The strong arms didn't let go, though.

"Sorry, didn't mean to scare you, but it was too good to pass up."

"Collin, you almost gave me a heart attack! Hey, Lacey, are you ready to go on the rides?"

"Yes, where's Riley?" she asked, looking around shyly. Lacey was dressed in jeans and a cute red shirt with a big black lacy heart in the center. Her black hair was pulled back into two pigtails, her natural curls forming perfect little ringlets.

"Riley's in the bathroom with his mom, he'll be right back. I like your shirt. Hearts are my favorite, you know." Collin had released me long enough for me to crouch down to Lacey's eye level while I talked to her. "Your hair sure is cute in those pigtails."

"Thank you. Collin did it." Lacey's crystal-blue eyes, so much like Collin's, finally looked up at me. She was still so shy but had at least warmed up to me a little. It was Riley who had won her over entirely, though.

I looked up at Collin. "Really? Collin put your hair in pigtails? Wow, I'm impressed."

He shrugged his shoulders. "It's better if it's out of her face. I can handle some pigtails, but that's about as far as it goes. None of those fancy braid things you girls do."

I stood back up to face him. "Still very impressive."

"RILEY!" Lacey yelled.

Turning, I could see Eileen coming around the corner holding Riley's hand, his bag over her shoulder. Riley pulled out of her grasp and ran the last few feet to us.

"WACEY!" He stopped just short of Lacey, and hugged her.

"Well, I guess there's no question that's Lacey, so you must be Collin. Very nice to meet you. I'm glad you guys could make it today."

Collin had reached over to shake Eileen's hand. "And you must be Eileen. Thanks for inviting us. Lacey's very excited. My dad and I brought her here back in November right after they got the Christmas stuff up, but we didn't stay very long, 'cause it got too cold and started to rain."

"Allright, so teacups next?" I asked.

"Sure, let's go. Come on, Lacey, we're going to go get in one of those big teacups and spin."

Collin pulled my hand into his while we stood in line. As we waited, Lacey and Riley debated which color teacup we were going to get in, at last narrowing it down to the green or purple. In the end, the only color left for us was red, and I wondered at first if they were going to be upset, but as we climbed in, Lacey declared that red was the best color anyway. We all crammed in, knees bumping against each other, the space very tight for three adults and two kids.

The ride got started and Collin pulled hard on the little wheel, sending us all into a high-speed spin very quickly. Riley and Lacey were both squealing with delight. Eileen was holding on to them so they wouldn't bash into each other. I was laughing but then had to focus on the center of the teacup and not look out at the spinning world around me. I could feel the queasiness starting.

"Ahh... Collin..."

"Yeah? Oh, geez, are you okay? You look a little green."

"Just need to slow it down a bit, please."

Collin let the wheel go, and the cup started to slow down to a more manageable speed. I was relieved when the ride came to a stop shortly after, but the kids were begging to go on it again.

Eileen helped Riley and Lacey out. I followed them, still feeling a little dizzy. Collin reached around me and steadied me as we walked toward the gate.

"Sorry, I forgot how easily I can get sick on the spinning rides."

He just chuckled. "It's okay. I'll remember that for next time. You're already getting color back in your face, so that's a good sign."

We got to the exit gate where Eileen and the kids waited for us, both of the little ones jumping up and down.

"Please, can we go again?" Lacey asked.

"Pwease? Pwease?" Riley chimed in.

"It's okay, I'll sit this one out; you guys go. I'll wait over by the stroller."

"Are you sure?" Eileen asked.

"Yes, go. They had fun, and this time Collin can spin it fast the entire time."

The four of them got back in line. The line had been short enough that they were able to get right back on, again in one of the red teacups. They waved after they got seated. Pulling out my camera, I shot a picture of them sitting in the teacup smiling. The ride got started, and I could see both of the kids laughing. Collin had the teacup spinning so fast they were like a blur passing by. Even Eileen was laughing. I knew it was good for her to get out and have a good time too.

I walked over to the exit with the stroller and waited for them to get out of the teacup. We then walked over to Alice in Wonderland. Lacey loved the caterpillars, and we ended up in a pink one. Eileen had squeezed in the front with Lacey and Riley, and that left the back for Collin and me. I climbed in first, and Collin slid in next to me. As we ventured down through the rabbit hole into the world of Wonderland, Collin placed his arm around me and pulled me against him. Leaning my head against his shoulder, I felt content. It was going to be a great day; one I knew I would never forget. In the front seat, Riley screamed with delight at the Cheshire cat, with his purple and blue stripes and moony, grinning face.

Once the ride was over, we collected the stroller, and Eileen led the way over to the Mad Hatter, where she proceeded to purchase Mickey ears hats with our names embroidered on them for each of us. Both Collin and I tried to pay for ours, but Eileen refused. After trying to slip money into her purse and getting it promptly returned to me, I let her finish paying.

By the time midafternoon rolled around, we had already ridden It's a Small World, been to Toontown, visited both Mickey and Minnie in their houses, had lunch in New Orleans Square, and were in line for Pirates of the Caribbean. Lacey had warmed up immediately to Eileen, and I could tell she was in seventh heaven with the attention Eileen gave her. Lacey had grabbed Eileen's hand and held it while we walked between rides and waited in lines. I was also discovering that Lacey could be quite the chatterbox. It warmed my heart, as I knew that Lacey needed a mother's attention. I looked up at Collin and could see he was thinking the same thing, his face marked with pain but also relief that she was truly having a great time.

I caught his eye, and he smiled. "She really likes Eileen. This is good for her. I'm so glad Eileen invited us."

"Yeah, me too. This is by far my favorite trip to Disneyland."

"Mine too."

Our boat arrived to take us through the waters of pirates, treasures, and battles. I worried a bit about the darkness on the ride and hoped the kids wouldn't get scared. Lacey was a little unsure of the drops, but Riley was fascinated, and after the ride was over, he spent most of the afternoon singing "yo ho, yo ho, a pirate's life for me!"

After pirates, we explored Tarzan's Treehouse and the Jungle Cruise. When we finally walked out of Adventureland, Lacey's little feet were getting tired, and Collin had been carrying her the last little bit, so we decided to rent her a stroller. Riley had already fallen asleep, and I was pretty sure Lacey would not be far behind, and sure enough, she hadn't been in the stroller more than ten minutes before she was fast asleep.

Eileen suggested that Collin and I hit some of the other rides while the kids were sleeping. The Matterhorn was first on our list; we found the end of the line and slowly began moving our way around the mountain. As we walked, Collin snagged my hand and interlinked it with his own.

"So, I have to ask, what's the story on Eileen?"

"You mean her background?"

"Yeah, how'd you meet her, that kind of thing."

"Her husband was in the military and was killed overseas a little over two years ago. He never got to meet Riley. Eileen grew up in Riverview, and after her husband was killed, she moved back to be near family and friends. Riley was only three months old at the time."

"Wow, that had to have been hard."

"Yeah, my aunt and Eileen have been friends for years. After Eileen moved back, she needed a babysitter, and I was available. I had just moved down here, and it worked out well. Eileen and I both were suffering over our losses. My being with her and Riley helped both of us. Babysitting helped keep me occupied, and Riley has been so much fun. Watching him grow and learn new things has been an amazing experience for me. I love kids, but I know one thing for sure, they are a lot of work and I'll be waiting to have my own for a long time!"

"Totally! Lacey can be quite a handful sometimes."

The line moved fairly quickly at the Matterhorn, but I hardly noticed. Collin's hand was still linked with mine; I could not get enough of the closeness. Every time he touched me, my stomach would turn topsy-turvy. Every nerve and all of my senses were on high alert. I felt alive and electrified, and I craved it more and more. Words were unnecessary; all we seemed to need was contact with each other.

Climbing into our bobsled, we ended up in the back car by ourselves. Collin climbed in first and I sat in front of him, leaning against his rock hard chest. His arms wrapped around me, and I nestled my hands on top of his. Soon we were off, climbing and twisting through the mountain. As it got cooler inside the artificial mountain, I was glad for Collin's warmth radiating through my cotton T-shirt. When we whipped around another corner, the Abominable Snowman appeared, and a scream ripped from my throat. I could feel the ripple of laughter as his chest moved behind me. I had been on this ride so many times, yet today I'd forgotten about the big white beast with the bright red eyes. The ride came to an end and we climbed out, Collin jumping out first and pulling me out beside him. We walked toward the exit and then around the mountain toward where Eileen was waiting for us.

Suddenly Collin pulled me into the shadows at the back of the mountain where we were slightly shielded from those walking past. I caught the intense smoldering of his eyes as he leaned down, ever so gently, and completely took control of my lips in a breath-taking kiss. I was overwhelmed by the intensity as it burned through my body, feeling it all the way to the tips of my toes. My body felt like it would melt into a puddle on the ground. My arms took on a life of their own as they reached up behind his head and my hands twisted in his hair.

Slowly Collin pulled away, but with my arms still linked around his neck, he didn't go far.

"I've been wanting to do that from the moment I saw you today."

"You can do that anytime. I'm not complaining."

Smiling, he pulled me next to him, and we started walking again, his arm slung around my lower back and settled comfortably at my waist. "We need to get back to Eileen before she wonders what happened to us."

Eileen saw us approaching and got up to move the strollers. "Well, did you guys have fun?"

Damn, my body was so traitorous! As I felt the blood rush to my face, I knew Eileen would see through the blush for what it was. "Yes, but I forgot about the Abominable Snowman and practically shattered Collin's eardrums screaming."

She chuckled, "Don't worry, that thing gets me every time. So where to next? The kids will probably be out for a while longer. Do you want to ride Space Mountain? They will probably be up by the time you're done, and we can eat at the pizza place that's right there."

Collin let go of my waist as he reached for Lacey's stroller. "Sounds like a plan to me."

"Eileen, are you sure you want to sit and wait? Collin and I can always come back another day."

"You guys are going. There's no reason not to."

It didn't take long to get over to Tomorrowland. Collin and I left Eileen with the strollers, and walked toward the entrance for Space Mountain. We passed by a huge polished concrete ball, or maybe it was some type of stone. It was huge, probably close to five feet in diameter. It was nestled in a well of water with water pouring over it. Kids were running around it laughing as they pushed it. The massive sphere would spin in all directions almost as though it were weightless. I knew Riley and Lacey would get a kick out of playing with it.

Entering the line for Space Mountain, I remembered being terrified of the ride as a child, crying all the way through the line, begging my parents not to make me go on it. Most times I would get worked up into such hysteria that, by the time we got to the loading area, one of them would walk me through and wait for everyone else to ride. To this day, I don't know why it frightened me so badly. Maybe it was the dark. I always had to have a night light on in my room when I was little. I pushed those memories aside. I didn't want to think about my family or the past. I wanted to focus on today, now, this time with Collin.

As we weaved through the chains that outlined our path, working our way through the line, Collin stole kisses here and there. Standing on the bridge area, we looked down, watching as the shuttles were taking off.

Collin had his arms around me, his chin nestled on the top of my head. I pulled out my camera and snapped a picture of us. Flipping the camera around, I checked the image on the back to make sure I didn't cut our heads off in the picture as I so often did. It was perfect. The shot captured the smiles on both of our faces; the blue lights of the ride as our backdrop made the intensity of Collin's eyes stand out even more vividly than usual. It was a keeper and would go into my scrapbook that I was beginning to put together.

We crept down the stairs until it was finally our turn to enter into the rocket ships and blast off into the darkness of the ride. The blackness was broken only by tiny sparkles of light as the ride sped along the track—up, down, side to side, the cold air breezing past my face. Way too quickly it was over, and we came to a screeching halt.

We exited the ride, and as we approached Eileen, I realized both Riley and Lacey were running around the large ball of stone, pushing it as it slid on its water base.

Lacey caught sight of Collin first. "Collin! Watch, I can move it all by myself!"

Proud of herself, Lacey pushed on the sphere, and it rolled to the right.

"Wow, Lacey, that's pretty cool."

"I can do it too!" Riley interjected as he pushed it to the left and the sphere shifted direction.

Eileen walked up. "Your timing is perfect. They've only been up for about ten minutes and have been completely entertained by this thing. Are you guys ready to eat?"

"Yes!" Riley and Lacey answered in unison.

"How about some pizza?"

"Yes!" they both agreed. Who wouldn't? You could never go wrong with pizza.

After dinner, we rode Autopia, the Finding Nemo Submarine, and Buzz Lightyear. Dusk had fallen, and the wind had started to pick up. Both Riley and Lacey seemed completely worn out. We decided it was time to call it a day and started walking back to the cars. As we moved through the park toward Main Street, we made one last stop at the castle to take some pictures. The lights had come on, and it was completely lit up. I felt like I was indeed a princess with my Prince Charming, in front of our castle, wishing that the magical day would never come to an end.

We returned Lacey's stroller and exited the park. Reaching the World of Disney store, we went inside for some souvenirs to add to our Mickey ears. By the time we walked out of the store, each kid had a bag full. Both of them ended up with a package of Mickey Mouse lollipops, Lacey had selected a Tinkerbell T-shirt and a Nemo stuffed animal, while Riley's choices were a Lightning McQueen T-shirt and a Buzz Lightyear spinning toy. I had found a white sleep shirt that had Mickey and Minnie on it kissing, the background a grid of interlinked gray hearts. It made me smile when I first saw it, and it would forever remind me of this trip with Collin.

Before we left the Disney experience altogether, we made one last stop at the ice cream shop, each of us getting an ice cream cone. After the creamy treats were finished, it was time to get on the tram. The tram ride back to the parking structure was unlike our trip in; everyone was silent. Lacey was leaning against Collin, and Riley was curled up in my lap, resting his head against my shoulder. Eileen maneuvered the stroller off the tram and unfolded it as Riley climbed back in.

"Eileen, we'll walk you guys up to your car. What level are you on?" Collin asked.

"Mickey Mouse. Riley was quite pleased with that."

"We ended up on Daisy."

Catching the elevator just before it shut, we all climbed in and rode it up to Mickey Mouse level. Eileen had gotten lucky so we had parked pretty close to the elevator. There were times I remember being here when I was younger and we'd ended up on the absolute farthest corner away from the escalators. Those were the days when the walk felt like it was miles, made worse when your feet were already aching from being on them all day.

Riley climbed into his car seat, and I figured he would be out before Eileen even got out of the parking structure. The stroller got loaded into the trunk, and I turned to say my goodbyes to Collin and Lacey.

"Bailey, if you want to drive home with Collin, go. I'm good with Riley."

"It's okay, Eileen, you don't need to drive home by yourself."

"No, really, go."

"Are you sure? My car is at your house. I can help you get everything inside when I pick it up."

"That would be great. Now go. Thanks for coming with me, all of you. It would have been really hard for me to bring Riley by himself, and this was way more fun for him."

Lacey quietly walked over to Eileen, and before anyone knew what she was doing, she threw her arms around Eileen's legs in a big hug. "Thanks, Mrs. Howard."

I could see the tears forming in Eileen's eyes. "You bet, Lacey. You can call me Eileen okay? And we'll have you come over soon to play with Riley, alright?"

"Okay." Lacey returned to Collin and grabbed his hand.

Giving Eileen a big smile, I thanked her and leaned in to kiss Riley goodbye. "'Night, buddy, I'll see you later. Okay?"

"Okay," Riley murmured sleepily.

I walked with Collin and Lacey back to the escalators to the Daisy level. Collin had not been as lucky as Eileen, and though he was not parked quite at the farthest corner possible, it was close. Lacey was riding piggyback on Collin, and I did not blame her one bit, poor thing. Her little feet had traversed a lot of area today.

When we finally reached Collin's car, I tossed our bags in the back while he helped Lacey get buckled in. As I'd expected. Lacey was asleep before we even got on the freeway. Collin pulled my hand in his, and they both rested over the console. We drove home with the music playing in the background, mostly quiet, with smoldering glances toward each other. Collin would occasionally squeeze my hand and then bring it up to his lips to kiss it softly. It could not have been a more perfect day.

CHAPTER SIX

~ Bailey ~

It was late, and I had just gotten home from spending the evening with Collin. Since our day at Disneyland, we'd spent some part of every day together. Like the previous nights, we had ended up at the lookout, sitting under the stars, talking and enjoying just being with each other. I was now curled up on my bed in my Disneyland sleep shirt. My window was open, and the breeze was slightly stirring the curtains.

I reached down to grab the book I'd been reading when my fingertips brushed along the edges of my journal. I slowly pulled it out. It had been so long since I had written anything in it. At one point, it had been a nightly ritual, something I loved to do. Writing had given me a freedom to just be myself, because it didn't matter what I wrote. I could be as serious or silly as I wanted. I flipped the pages until I reached the last entry from two years ago.

February 4

I'm at my aunt and uncle's house now. It still feels like a nightmare. How could this have happened to me?? What did I do to deserve this? Why did I survive?? Mom, Dad, how could you leave me alone like this? It's not fair... Brandon and Brooke, I miss you so so much. I can't do this, I don't know if I can get through this.

Closing my eyes to stop the pain that washed over me, my eyes filled with tears. This was why I hadn't picked up the journal for so long. Amazingly, though, the crushing grief that I had felt for the past two years now felt almost bearable. I guess it was true that time did help heal, but I was pretty sure that it had a lot to do with Collin. Maybe it was time to pick up the pen again.

March 27

It's been a long time since I've been able to write in here. The best thing possible has happened: I've met the most amazing guy. He makes me feel alive again. It's like everything around me seems to stop when he's there. He makes me feel special, and for the first time I'm actually glad that I did survive. Maybe there was a reason I made it. For so long, I've lived with the guilt of being the survivor. I know deep down Mom and Dad would want me to be happy and to move on with my life, and I know Mom especially would love Collin.

I try not to let the fear of something bad looming on the horizon affect me and wish I could just shove it where it would never come out again. But for me, I know life and reality can be harsh. Maybe, though, I've paid my dues and it's time for me to be happy again? That can't be too much to ask, can it? For now I just want to enjoy the giddy feeling and the excitement that I'm experiencing.

So I'm starting anew, and for now, I'm writing about the good times. Maybe it will all end up being a silly crush, but for now it feels real, and it's fun.

It's like he completely understands me. When we're apart, I long for the time to fly by so that we can be together again.

The first time he kissed me, I could feel the jolt all the way down to my toes, as his gentle lips touched mine. It was better than I'd ever imagined, my first kiss. It felt so right, like we were made for each other. It feels weird. Part of me thinks there is no way it can last, that nothing can be this perfect, not in my world, but I can still hope that maybe...just maybe...my luck might be changing.

I won't wait so long to write again. It feels good. For now I guess it's time for bed. It's late, and in the morning I'll have little Riley to entertain.

Sliding the pen back into the journal, I set it aside. It was crazy how just writing a few words on paper made me feel so much better, like a huge burden was lifted from my shoulders. I wondered again how a few short weeks could totally turn my life upside down in a good way. I flipped off the light and slipped under my sheets. I was just starting to doze when my phone buzzed.

Collin: Goodnight baby
Bailey: night Collin :) sweet dreams

Smiling, I set the phone back on my nightstand.

~ *Collin* ~

Driving through the streets, images of Bailey were running through my head. Her gray-blue eyes were sometimes so intense they were a deep green. There were times when she looked at me, and it was almost like she could peer into my soul. I wondered if she realized what effect she had on me. The perfume she always wore lingered in my car; often the intoxicating sweet vanilla smell even lingered on my clothes, as if her presence was still there when she was gone.

In some ways, it troubled me that a girl could get so under my skin. I was always in control of my emotions, in control of any situation. With Bailey, however, I felt like I was totally spinning with no way to stop. My dad was so unpredictable, and I knew that at any time he could decide to move again. Usually just that possibility alone caused me to keep my distance with girls, having fun but never getting attached. With Bailey it was so different: I was pulled to her like a magnet. It didn't matter that each day I told myself that our relationship was moving too fast. I seemed to do just the opposite of what my head was telling me to do. It was as if a force stronger than my will was guiding the next move. It was not a comfortable feeling for me.

There was something so fragile and broken about her that made me just want to "fix" her, help her heal. I wished I could erase the pain she had been living with. I tried to focus on Lacey, knowing that she should be my priority, but Bailey was constantly creeping into my heart, so fast I felt sometimes like the life was being sucked out of me when I had to leave her. I knew that somehow I had to try and keep some distance between us before I was totally under her spell. What I didn't know was how I would be able to actually follow through with it.

Parking in front of my house, I cut the engine. Grabbing the keys and my cell phone, I climbed out of the Camaro and walked up the sidewalk to the house, texting Bailey as I walked. Her response, as always, brought a smile to my face. Reaching the front door, I unlocked it and went in. It was late, and I was surprised to find my dad still up in the living room.

"Hey, Dad, you're up late."

"We're having company arrive on Friday. They are planning on staying for a week. I was trying to get things ready."

"Who's coming?"

"The Porters."

"We haven't seen them in a couple of years. Why did they decide to come visit now?"

"Timing, mostly since they are closer to us now and the kids are on spring break, they thought it would be nice to come for a visit and a small vacation."

"Guess I'm losing my room for the week?"

"Yeah, sorry. Shane and Lynette will stay in your room, Savannah and Ashley can stay with Lacey."

"That's all right; I'll survive on the couch."

"Lynette says that Savannah is very excited to see you, although I'm not supposed to pass that information on."

"Ah, nice. Savannah is just a friend, Dad. Nothing more than that. I mean, we grew up together; she's like another little sister."

"Okay, whatever you say, but you guys were always hanging out together. You went to some dances together."

"Who was I supposed to hang out with? Our families were always together, and Ashley is a lot younger. We went to the dances as friends, that's it."

"I'm just saying it never looked like you didn't like hanging out together."

"Dad, I'm kinda seeing someone else right now, okay. Don't push it."

"Oh. Well, this is the first time I'm hearing anything about that. Who is she?"

"Her name is Bailey Walsh. She's the one Lacey and I went to Disneyland with the other day. You really don't pay much attention to anything I tell you, do you?"

"You didn't mention you were 'kinda seeing' her."

"Yeah, well, I am, okay?" I went upstairs stopping at Lacey's door, I peeked inside to check on her. Her pink princess comforter had slipped down so I walked over to pull it back up over her shoulders. In her arms she clutched her new Nemo stuffed animal, a tendril of black hair curled over her face. Carefully, I pushed it aside and leaned over to kiss her forehead. Turning, I left her room silently, leaving the door cracked.

Reaching my room, I tossed my jacket over the chair. Most things in my room were organized and in their proper spot, but a few lingering articles of clothing were tossed carelessly on the floor. I kicked aside the sweatshirt I had worn yesterday as I pulled off my shoes.

"Well, this should be an interesting week," I mumbled to myself.

Savannah and I had always had gotten along really well. She was a senior in high school just like me, and I did look forward to seeing her again. In fact, I had missed her laughter over the past couple of years. We sent text messages to each other every once in a while, and a few e-mails, but nothing more than just friends stuff. I wondered if things would be weird after not seeing each other for two years. For most of our lives, we had lived just a block apart. Our dads had been roommates in college, and our moms had become best friends. Our families had always hung out together and several times took vacations together. It had been like that until my mom had abruptly left.

Savannah's mom, Lynette, had been a godsend those first weeks, helping to take care of Lacey. Dad had remained in a state of shock, thinking that she would be back. Eventually he couldn't take it anymore. The daily reminders of all the good times ended up being too much for him, and he had packed Lacey and I up and moved.

Dad and Shane had kept in contact over the past couple of years, talking almost every week, but things had changed, and they would probably never be as close as they had once been. Shortly after our family had moved the first time, Lynette had been offered a great job in Las Vegas, and they had relocated as well.

I finished getting ready for bed and fell into a troubled sleep. Tossing and turning most of the night, my dreams were uncertain, and none of them made any sense. Pink was spilling across the sky before I was able to finally slip into an undisturbed sleep.

A HEALING HEART

~ Savannah ~

Friday morning dawned warm and sunny in Las Vegas. I was up early and anxious to get on the road. I had carefully laid out my clothes for the day and had spent hours packing just the right outfits for our trip to Southern California to visit the McKennas. My heart beat faster just thinking about seeing Collin again. It had been too long since I had seen him. Ever since the McKenna family had moved to Southern California, just a few hours' drive away from us, I had been trying to convince my parents to go for a visit. Something had always come up, but now that the time was here, it seemed so unreal. I wondered how I would be able to survive the drive.

My crush on Collin started years ago. I knew that one day, when the time was right, we would officially be boyfriend and girlfriend. My dreams had almost come true during our freshman year of high school. Collin and I had gone to a couple of school dances and we had even kissed several times. Just when things were going good, all of my plans had gone up in smoke when Collin's mom took off and his dad abruptly moved the family away.

For the past two years, my only contact with Collin had been a few phone calls and sporadic text messages, most of them just casual "how are you doing" sort of messages. I cherished each time I was able to talk to him, wishing for the day when I'd be able to see him again.

The sense of failure that I felt was intense after his family had moved away. I did not fail at things that I set my mind to. I was determined that Collin would be mine one day, and I felt that I'd been pretty patient over the last couple of years. It didn't matter what obstacle lay in the way of that goal, I was bound and determined to have Collin. I knew we were perfect for each other, meant for each other. I just had to have the opportunity to make Collin realize it as well. What I needed now was some time and a little bit of luck.

~ *Collin* ~

Arriving home from work Friday evening, I noticed a strange car in the driveway and assumed it must belong to the Porters. With a sigh, I got out and walked toward the front door. Though I was looking forward to seeing them, I'd been hoping to get home before they were here so that I could leave right away and pick up Bailey. Now I would have to take a few minutes at least and be polite. I quickly texted Bailey, letting her know that I was running late. Laughter from inside greeted me as I opened the front door. Walking silently through the house, I reached the kitchen where everyone was gathered. Lynette noticed me first.

"Hey, Collin! It's so good to see you. Wow, you've grown, but handsome as ever! Come over here and give me a hug."

"Hi, Lynette."

Lynette had almost been like a second mom to me, and it was good to see her again. I went over and gave her a warm hug. Shane was next with a strong handshake and a pat on the back.

"Hi, kid. You're looking good, almost taller than your dad now."

"Thanks."

Looking around, I noticed Lacey curled up on the couch next to Ashley.

"Hi, Ash."

"Hey, Collin."

Savannah had been sitting next to Ashley and had quickly come over to the kitchen. Stopping just short of me, with a slight hesitation, she leaned over for a hug, "Hi, Collin. It's been a long time."

"Hi, Savannah. Yeah, it's been a while."

Releasing Savannah, I pulled out a kitchen chair and sat down next to Lynette. Savannah followed, picking the chair closest to me while Dad and Shane left the kitchen and walked into the family room.

"So, Lynette, what are you guys planning to do this week?" I asked.

"Well, we've been thinking Disneyland, maybe Sea World, or Universal Studios, the beach. Nothing is really set in stone yet. Your dad says you're off on spring break this week as well."

"I've been out this week and have next week off too. I've been working most days, though, with only a few days off. I was just at Disneyland the other day with Lacey, so you'll probably want to do that trip without me. Tomorrow a bunch of kids from school are going down to the beach."

Savannah piped up, "Hey, can I come?"

"Sure. I'm not sure who all is going, but you can join us."

"Cool! I haven't been to the beach in years."

"Well, I hate to run, but I've got plans tonight and need to change clothes. I already moved most of my stuff out of my room for you guys, so make yourselves at home. I'll be back later."

~ *Savannah* ~

Collin stood up and left the kitchen. He was taller and had filled out since I'd last seen him. I could feel his strength when we hugged. His cologne, so subtle, was the same brand that I remembered. My pulse had raced in his embrace, but he seemed distant. This was not what I'd thought would happen when we saw each other again. It was like I barely existed. How could he just run out like that? We hadn't seen each other for over two years and that was it? "Hi, Savannah, bye, Savannah." I'd expected him to be more excited to see me.

The drive from Vegas had seemed to drag on and on, and then when we had finally arrived, I'd been so disappointed that Collin wasn't even here to greet us. I'd patiently waited for him to get home from work thinking we'd be able to spend the evening together getting caught up, but it looked like that wasn't going to happen either. So far, things were not going as I'd planned.

I was still sitting at the table with my mom when I heard Collin's footsteps racing down the stairs, and in an instant he was out the door. He didn't even come in to say goodbye. I wondered where he was going in such a hurry.

Trying not to let it bother me, I focused on tomorrow. He had promised to take me to the beach tomorrow, so maybe it would be different. Having him all to myself on the way down to the beach would be a good start. There would be plenty of time to get reacquainted. I only had a week here with Collin and I needed to make the best of it.

A HEALING HEART

~ *Bailey* ~

The phone buzzing brought me back from my daydream. I glanced down and read the text: Collin was running late. A bit out of the usual for him, but maybe they held him at work. We were just going out for ice cream tonight. The plan was to be back home early since tomorrow we were going down to the beach early in the morning to join a bunch of other kids from school. Mia and Natasha had gotten back today from their skiing trip, and I was anxious to see them and update them on the week's adventures. I'd been texting them through the week, but reception where they were was not always reliable.

Leaving my room, I went downstairs to wait for Collin to arrive. The house was quiet; my aunt and uncle weren't home. I enjoyed the quiet most of the time, but sometimes it was almost too quiet. I remembered how irritated I got when my brother and sister would run around the house screaming at each other. "He touched me/she looked at me." There was always something they were fighting about. I would try to ignore the screaming, wishing so many times they would stop. Now, I would give about anything in the world to hear them screaming at each other again. I shook my head to clear it. I knew I needed to stop dwelling on the things I couldn't change, but still, the thoughts would creep into my head.

Collin pulled up a few minutes later. I guess he wasn't running as late as he had thought. I hurried out, eager to see him. He met me at the passenger door. I wrapped my arms around him and looked up into his sparkling blue eyes. His hands lightly touched the sides of my face as he leaned down and kissed me in greeting.

Pulling away slightly, he held me a bit longer with his chin nestled on the top of my head. We seemed to fit each other perfectly.

"I missed you. It's been a long day!"

"I missed you too. I thought you were running late." Stepping aside, Collin opened the door for me and I slid in.

After starting the car, he turned to me. "I wasn't sure how long it would take at my house. We have company."

"Oh, who?" This was the first time he had mentioned having company at his house. A sense of uneasiness washed over me. As quickly as it came, I tried to shove it aside.

"Old family friends. We used to live down the block from them. I've known them all my life. My dad and Shane were old college roommates."

I was overreacting; my stomach started to settle down a bit. "That's cool. How long are they here for?"

"A week. Their kids are on spring break, so they're planning on doing the tourist thing: Disneyland, Sea World, all those kind of things."

"Kids? How old are they?"

"Savannah is a senior, and Ashley is eleven."

The knots were suddenly back in my stomach. "Oh."

Collin's eyes darted to me, "What do you mean 'Oh'?"

Breaking away from his searching gaze, I looked out at the front windshield. "Nothing. Never mind." I felt his hand turn my head back toward his.

"That doesn't sound like nothing. What's wrong?"

I let out a deep sigh. "Is Savannah somebody special to you?"

"I grew up with her, we were best friends. Yeah, she's someone special, but she's like a sister to me."

"That's it? Just like a sister?"

"Bailey, yes, that's it. I haven't seen her in two years. She's like another sister, okay."

"Okay." I smiled hesitantly at him, but the knots were still lodged in my stomach.

"Where am I right now? With you. I got out of the house as quickly as I could, to see you. Okay?"

I knew he was right; I pushed aside the uneasiness and settled in to enjoy the next few hours with him. We shared a hot fudge sundae while sitting on the outdoor patio of the food court. We laughed as little kids ran in and out of the water feature located in the center. The evening was starting to cool, but the kids didn't seem to mind. As the sun set that night, the clouds in the sky turned deep red and orange. So beautiful and bright, it almost looked like the sky was on fire. The saying "Red sky at night, sailor's delight" ran through my head. It was a good omen that the weather tomorrow would be great, and a day at the beach with Collin would be like heaven.

CHAPTER SEVEN

~ *Savannah* ~

I was up early Saturday morning, carefully picking out my best bikini, my shortest shorts, and my favorite tank top. My top stopped just before it reached the waistline of my shorts. As I moved, glimpses of my tanned, slim waist were visible, showing off my new belly button piercing. My parents had been horrified when they had discovered the piercing. I was eighteen, though, so they really couldn't say much to me about it.

This morning I decided to leave my long blonde hair down and carefully applied my makeup to accent my deep brown eyes. Reviewing the finished product in the full-length mirror, I was satisfied with my appearance and went downstairs to meet Collin.

Collin sat at the table eating a bowl of cereal; he glanced up as I came into the room. "Hey, Savannah, you ready?"

"Yes, whenever you are." I was a bit miffed that he didn't seem to notice me except for a slight glance in my direction. This was not the reaction I was hoping, or expecting, to get. I wondered what must be on his mind that would cause him to be so preoccupied. I hoped this wasn't an indication of how the entire week was going to be!

"Do you want breakfast? I'm almost done and need to grab the beach towels. I already loaded the beach chairs that we have and an ice chest; everyone's bringing something. A couple of the kids left early this morning to save us a fire pit."

"Cool, let me grab some warmer clothes then for later. It sounds like we're going to be down there for a while. I'm not really a breakfast person, so I'm good."

Leaving the kitchen, I raced upstairs grinning. Maybe all was not lost—an evening at the beach with Collin could be quite exciting. A walk along the sand or watching the sunset would be cool. There were several possibilities that could be a lot of fun. Rummaging through my suitcase, I located my capri sweats and matching sweatshirt. Tossing them into the bag with my other clothes, I went back downstairs.

Collin was waiting for me at the front door. "I've got everything loaded if you're ready to go."

"I'm ready, let's go!"

I followed Collin to his car and got into the front seat as he went around to the driver's side. Collin started the car, and we pulled away from the curb.

"Nice car, by the way."

"Thanks. I got a good deal on it but had to do some work to it to get it to run right. The previous owner was going through a divorce and didn't want to deal with it."

"Um-hmm. So isn't the freeway the other direction? Where are we going?"

"Oh, sorry, I have one stop to make first. We need to pick up Bailey."

"Bailey? Who's Bailey?"

"I guess you could say she's my girlfriend, although we've not officially called it that yet."

My heart stopped. "Your what?" I could barely spit the words out.

Collin glanced sideways at me, "My girlfriend."

"That's what I thought you said. When did this happen? How come you haven't mentioned her before?" I tried to keep my voice even, but inside I was seething. How and when could this have happened?

He shrugged. "A few weeks ago. The topic just didn't come up. She's great. I'm sure you'll really like her." He flashed me a big grin that only made the matter a hundred times worse.

Forcing a smile, I did the only thing I could right now, which was to agree. It was a good thing I hadn't eaten breakfast or I would have probably needed to puke. This was a major setback, but not impossible to overcome. I would just have to change my tactics a bit and refocus. Failure was not an option.

~ *Bailey* ~

I was finishing packing for the beach, mentally going through my checklist to make sure I didn't forget anything. The food I was responsible for bringing was already downstairs waiting by the door. All I needed now was to grab my sunblock and baseball hat. My skin did not fare well in the sun and I didn't want to come home looking like a red lobster. I could hear the faint rumble of Collin's car coming up the street, so I grabbed my belongings by the front door and walked outside.

Collin pulled his car up to the curb and I almost stopped on the sidewalk as I noticed a stunning blonde girl sitting in the front seat. Savannah? It had to be. She was coming with us? Great. Somehow the excitement of the trip quickly evaporated. I couldn't understand why Collin hadn't mentioned that she was joining us today. I forced myself to plaster a smile on my face and continued walking toward the car. Collin jumped out and reached me quickly, grabbing my bags and carrying them to the back hatch.

After he had finished loading the items, he leaned down and brushed a light kiss across my lips. "Morning."

"Morning," I replied, then without skipping a beat, I couldn't help but ask, "So, is that Savannah?"

"Yeah, I asked her last night if she wanted to come with us. I thought she might have fun with everyone."

"Oh. Okay."

Collin opened the passenger door, his other arm lightly wrapped around my waist. We stepped aside as Savannah got out.

"Bailey, this is my friend Savannah. Savannah, this is Bailey."

"Hi," we both said in unison.

I knew we were each measuring the other one up. Savannah was absolutely gorgeous: a little shorter than me; long blonde hair, perfectly brushed back; flawless face; deep, chocolate brown eyes; angelic features; and slight dimples in her cheeks. There was no way I could compare to her. Her perfect body was set off with very skimpy jean shorts and a tank top that fit her tightly, leaving little to the imagination.

Savannah was the first to break the silence. "Here, let me move the seat up for you so you can climb in back."

I was not expecting that. I immediately knew I shouldn't underestimate this angelic creature in the front seat. I got the distinct impression that she wasn't much of an angel. I glanced quickly to Collin to see if he would correct her, but he said nothing, seemingly oblivious to the tension crackling between Savannah and I. Could he really not see through this ploy? I wasn't really surprised, though. Instinct told me that Savannah could twist anyone she wanted around her little finger.

"Ah, thanks." Two could play this game; I would just have to be quicker on the way home. I climbed into the tiny backseat. This was not the ride down to the beach I had been anticipating. I had barely gotten my knees adjusted when the seat came flying backward, crushing me further.

"Oh, sorry, wrong way. Let me fix that."

"It's okay," I muttered.

Finally the seat moved forward enough so that my knees were not jammed up to my chin. I was glad I couldn't see her face in the mirror: it was going to be a long drive.

Surprisingly, the trip down to the beach was not as awful as I had thought it was going to be. Collin kept the conversation going between the three of us. I was pretty sure he was unaware of how Savannah tried to isolate me. She was good; I would give her that. Her subtle changes in subjects and the light touches to Collin's shoulder had me gritting my teeth. The jealousy that coursed through me was intense, unlike anything I'd ever felt before. I really needed to try to get things under control before I snapped and said or did something I might regret later. From the little that Collin had told me I knew they went way back, and for now I'd give her the respect I'd give any of Collin's friends, but only so far. I also wasn't willing to be walked all over. I expected the same amount of respect in return.

We pulled into the beach parking lot and were lucky enough to find a spot pretty close to the fire pit area that our friends had been able to reserve. As we got out of the car, I caught sight of Mia and Natasha already walking in our direction.

"Hey Bailey, Collin, glad you guys made it. Um...who's this?" Mia, never the shy one, cut right to the point.

"Hi, Mia, this is an old family friend, Savannah. Her family is staying with us for the week. I thought she might have a good time with everyone today," Collin explained.

I could see Mia's eyebrow twitch up just slightly as she looked at Savannah and then at me. "Oh, hey, Savannah. Glad you could join us. I'm Mia."

"Hi, Mia, nice to meet you."

Mia, slipping her hand out of Savannah's, motioning next to her, "And this is Natasha."

"Hi, Natasha."

"So where are you from anyways?"

"Las Vegas."

"Come on, let's introduce you to everyone else. We're all over here. There are still a few others who should be here later."

Collin had emptied out the hatch, and we all grabbed our beach supplies and followed Mia into the soft, warm sand.

Collin and I brought up the rear, dropping back a little bit from the other three as we followed.

"Sorry you had to sit in the back. I didn't realize that she'd stay in the front seat."

"It's okay. She's your guest for the week. I'll survive." I tried to use my most convincing smile.

"Bailey, it's not like that, I promise."

"Yeah, sure. That's not the impression I got from her."

"Oh, come on, you're reading into things. We're just friends. I swear she's like a sister to me."

"Do you have eyes? She's like a model, Collin. I can't even come close to comparing to that."

He stopped me in my tracks and dropped everything he had in his hands, "Bailey, look at me." His hands gripped my upper arms. I glanced up into his eyes; they had taken on an icy tint. "You are beautiful, and you mean more to me right now than I'd really care to admit. Don't sell yourself short. You're the one that holds my heart, not Savannah. You have nothing to worry about with her."

My heart melted right on the spot. I felt slightly foolish, but oh, so relieved. "Okay, I believe you. I'm just saying, I don't think that's the way she feels."

"Point taken. But I still think you're reading into things."

Collin picked up the items that he'd discarded in the sand, and we finished our hike to the fire pit. Someone had already set up a canopy, and a table with food had been laid out. Ice chests were sitting on the ground; blankets and chairs were spread out. There were already almost a dozen kids from school there. We settled our towels and bags next to Mia and Natasha. Quinn had come up and had already hauled Collin off to help bring more firewood over. I was left introducing Savannah to the rest of the kids from school.

Several of the guys flocked around Savannah and were trying to outdo each other for her attention. I noticed, though, that she was constantly searching for Collin. I knew deep down my intuition was right. I couldn't let my guard down around her. As innocently as she was playing the game right now, I knew she wanted Collin, but I had no intention of letting her get her hooks in him.

Relaxing for a moment, I was able to take in my surroundings. I always loved the tranquility of the beach. The sun was bright and warm; the salty sea breeze was blowing white puffy clouds across the sky. It was indeed a beautiful day for a beach trip. I wouldn't enjoy the sand clinging to everything it touched, but it was a small price to pay.

I sat on a blanket while Collin finished helping Quinn with the firewood. Mia and Natasha were in their beach chairs drilling me with questions about my week and the beautiful stranger that had come with us.

"Did you know he was bringing her today?" Mia asked.

"No. I knew he had company, but I didn't realize she was coming until they got to my house to pick me up."

"Damn, that sucks. Sorry, Bailey."

"It's okay, Tasha. Collin swears she's only a friend. I think she was pretty shocked to see me too."

"Uh-huh, well, I'll tell you one thing, I wouldn't trust her as far as I could throw her. You better keep alert with her around."

"I know, Mia. I came to that conclusion the moment I set eyes on her."

"Well, you've got us here today for backup. We'll help keep her busy and out of your hair."

"Thanks, guys, you're the best!"

We were interrupted by Collin's voice. "So, is this just girl time right now, or am I allowed to join?"

"You're welcome here anytime, Collin." Mia smiled sweetly. "Have a seat."

I turned to Collin and gave him a bright smile. "Hey, since you're back now, can you finish spraying my back with the sunscreen? I really don't want to fry today."

"How bad could that really be? I promise to come over and rub aloe vera gel on you every couple of hours," Collin replied.

I couldn't help but laugh. "Thanks, but I'd rather not turn into a crispy critter It's too painful."

"Yeah, you're probably right. Come here. Let's get you sprayed, then we'll go down to the water."

Collin finished with the sunscreen, deeming me "completely protected" with my SPF of 70 everywhere. He grabbed my hand and we walked off into the deep sand toward the water, our hands entwined. For the time being, Savannah was forgotten, and it was just Collin and me. We reached the embankment near the water, and he pulled me down to sit in front of him on the sand. I leaned back against his warm chest as he wrapped his arms around me. With my fingers laced over his hands, we sat there watching the waves crash and wash up over the wet sand.

"Mmm...this is nice," Collin exhaled over the top of my head.

"Yes, absolutely perfect."

Sitting in silence my mind drifted. I thought back to the day at the park when Collin had only briefly mentioned his mom. He never talked about what had happened to her. I tilted my head back to look up at him. "I have a question."

His blue eyes sparkled as he grinned at me. "Okay, what is it?"

I shifted so I could see his face better, hoping that I wasn't going to shatter our good time, but I'd been totally open with him. It was only fair that he do the same with me.

"What happened with your mom? Why did she leave?"

Collin's gaze drifted from mine as he looked out over the glistening water. His body tensed and I was worried he was going to keep me shut out. When his eyes turned back to me I could see the hurt in them.

"I don't really like talking about her."

"Please Collin. I want to know the good and the bad, that's what relationships are, give and take."

"My mom wasn't really a mom, Bailey, not like yours was or even your aunt. My dad loved her more than anything, but she was always selfish, never satisfied, always looking for something bigger, something better. I guess she loved us, in whatever fashion she could. My dad hung on to what he could, he tried to make it work. He was always trying to please her.

"Then she got pregnant with Lacey. My dad was so excited when they found out it was going to be a girl. He was so sure that the new baby would be good for my mom, that it would be that missing piece she was always looking for. She would have a little girl to love. Lacey was born, and she's amazingly almost a spitting image of my mom—same hair color, facial structure, and eyes. Instead of bonding with her, my mom wanted nothing to do with her. The doctors said she had postpartum depression, and that she'd come out of it. But she never did; it got worse and worse. My dad and I were the ones taking care of Lacey while she was off shopping or doing whatever whim drove her next.

"When Lacey was eighteen months old, my mom packed up all her stuff and left. It ripped my dad apart. Part of him died that day. He's never really been the same since. Now, he mostly keeps his distance, working all the time. We always have what we need— food, clothes, babysitters for Lacey—but the one thing Lacey needs the most, the love of both of her parents, she won't ever have. I try to make up for that the best I can. Lacey is so shy, so afraid of new people, new environments. We never stay very long in one place. As soon as she starts feeling comfortable, we end up leaving again. I've begged my dad for us to stay in one place, but I think, in some ways, it's his way of coping, of running away from everything."

"You had to grow up quick. Taking care of Lacey and all. Not much of a chance for you to have a childhood either. I can see how attached she is to you. It all makes more sense now."

"I'm the lucky one. At least I had a mostly normal childhood. We stayed in one place during those years, I had my friends, did normal boy things. Lacey hasn't had that. She deserves that."

I looked at him and saw the strength, the unbending loyalty to his little sister. Now I knew why he seemed years older than just a senior in high school. The carefree abandon that most teenagers had wasn't present. It had been stripped from him years ago with the burden of taking care of his sister, and yet he didn't resent it. It made me fall for him even more.

The pain and heartache I'd lived with since the accident had blinded me for so long, but little by little that blindfold felt like it was lifting from me and that there was hope that life could be happy again.

"Thanks for telling me," I told him.

"My past has been a cakewalk compared to what you've endured. You are stronger than I think you realize."

I highly doubted that; we had both dealt with heartache, just in different forms. I settled back into his warm arms with the cool, salty air blowing over us.

~ *Savannah* ~

I was left at the fire pit, rage burning inside of me as I watched Collin walk with Bailey down to the water. Trying to ignore them, I focused my attention on the boy talking next to me. What was his name? Brett? No. Brent? No. Brad—yeah, that sounded right; it must be Brad. I nodded absently as he continued to ramble on about something, I think he was talking about football. Brad was handsome with his short blond hair and blue eyes. He was tall, very tan, and athletic, a typical Southern California teenager. I really wasn't interested in Brad—my interest lay elsewhere—but maybe he could be useful. Test the waters a bit, maybe I could spark a little jealousy in Collin. It was worth a shot, and at this point I had nothing to lose.

I couldn't understand what Collin saw in Bailey; she was nothing special. I knew, though, that I needed to be careful about how I handled things with Collin. The wrong move could backfire very quickly.

Turning toward Brad, I gave him one of my stunning smiles that showed off my perfect white teeth that I had spent nights bleaching. I could see my smile had the desired effect on him, so I knew I hadn't lost my touch. I just needed to figure out how to get the same reaction out of Collin. Focused on my goal for the day, I leaned over to touch Brad lightly on his shoulder, which was bare and muscled. To Brad's delight, I oohed and ahhed over how strong he was. Boys could be so predictable. Just a little stroking to their ego and they were like putty in my hands. Collin was going to be a challenge, but it would make the end reward even sweeter.

I knew from the little bit of conversation that I'd been paying attention to that Brad was the quarterback for the football team. He was talented enough that he'd even been awarded a college scholarship for the fall. As I sat there beside Brad, my mind wandered and I began planning how I would disentangle Bailey from Collin. Really, I thought to myself, how hard could it be?

~ *Bailey* ~

The day had flown by, most of the guys playing football and surfing while the girls laid out in the warm sun tanning. Collin and I walked along the beach together, picking up the few seashells that we came across. The sun was beginning to set over the water, tinting the sky with streams of pink, yellow, and orange. Together we watched as it finally dipped past the water and vanished.

Walking back to the campfire, my head rested comfortably on Collin's shoulder. His arm was wrapped around my waist. As bad as the morning had started, it really had been a nice, peaceful day. Savannah seemed to be caught up with Brad, which allowed me to let my guard down a little. Maybe I had overreacted a bit. Collin, although friendly with Savannah, had not appeared to be overly attentive toward her. She would only be here for a week; maybe it wouldn't be so bad.

Reaching the rest of our group, I noticed that they had already brought out the hot dogs and were roasting them over the fire. Sodas were set out on the tables and bags of chips were next to the plates and napkins. Mia and Natasha were sitting with Alex and Matt, both juniors and members of the football and basketball teams. Mia and Alex had gone out a couple of times over the past couple of months and seemed to enjoy each other's company. I thought they would make a cute couple: both very outspoken and athletic.

Collin and I grabbed our food and sat with the four of them. Before I could even take my first bite, Savannah was settling in on the other side of Collin. Brad sauntered up behind her carrying two plates of food and sat next to her, carefully handing her a plate and a diet Coke.

"Thanks, Brad, you're such a sweetie."

I almost choked on my food. Good grief; the comment was so forced and overdone. Glancing around, I noticed that only Mia and Natasha were rolling their eyes. Collin had noticed my slight cough, though, and was looking at me intently to make sure I was indeed okay.

"I'm fine. Food just went down the wrong track."

"Okay, I wasn't sure if I was going to have to start pounding on your back or something."

Smiling warmly, "No, I'm good, but thanks."

We finished eating our food, all the while chatting about the seniors' plans for the fall. Some of them were planning on attending college, while a few of the others had decided to work for a while and then figure out what they wanted to do with the rest of their lives. I realized that Collin and I had never really talked about what his plans were for the fall. My heart skipped slightly; I hoped that he wasn't planning on attending some faraway college. Now that it had come up, it was a topic I was anxious to ask him about.

I watched as the smoke from the fire pit trailed across the darkened sky. The stars were beginning to appear, and the crash of the waves pounding the beach was a constant soothing background. As the salty, sticky breeze tangled through my hair, I breathed in deeply, just enjoying the calm and letting my thoughts wander.

The fire pit crackled and brought my attention back to the present. Glancing around our group, I realized that Alex had grabbed one of the bags of marshmallows and a couple of hangers. He easily unfolded them into skewer sticks, placed them in the fire to burn off the coating and then passed them around our circle. Laughter floated through the group as several of the marshmallows that others were holding quickly burst into flames. The outside of the marshmallow scorched to a burnt crisp, falling into the fire.

I held out the wire with my marshmallow near the flames, but not where it would catch fire. Mine was turning a nice, light caramel color as the heat blistered the exterior of the white mushy goodness. I was a pro at toasting marshmallows; my family had gone camping together a lot, and marshmallow roasting had always been one of my favorite activities.

My eyes darted over at Savannah; she was clinging to Brad's shoulder as he attempted to roast two marshmallows at the same time. I was just glad she seemed to be leaving Collin alone. As she sat there, she looked so perfect; her hair did not have a strand out of place, and I wondered how that could be after spending an entire day in the breeze. Her clothes were coordinated, and revealing almost to the point of being slutty. Hoochie mama, that's what Mia would call her. Yet Savannah was able to pull off the entire look with it simply enhancing her curves. It was hard not to wonder how Collin could not be attracted to her. I couldn't wait until she went back home. My marshmallow was finished, and I pulled it away from the heat, allowing it to cool off just a little before sticking it in my mouth.

Collin reached for my arm and began pulling me up from the blanket that we were sitting on. "Come on, let's go for a walk."

Following, with my hand gripped tightly in his, I swore I could feel angry eyes boring into my back. I tried to ignore the shiver that immediately coursed down my spine, causing the hair to stand on end at my neck.

Slipping into an easy stride down to the water's edge, we walked hand in hand along the cold packed sand. The water occasionally lapped against our feet; the moon was full and bright and cast silvery shadows as we walked. It felt like a dream, one I never wanted to wake from. It was then that I realized that I had been able to sleep through the night for the past couple of weeks now without being tormented by my nightmares. I knew without a doubt I had Collin's presence to thank for that. Collin's voice broke through my wandering musings.

"Penny for your thoughts."

The comment caught me off guard, and I almost stopped in my tracks, forcing air down into my lungs. Collin noticed the paleness of my face in the moonlight and turned to me, alarmed. "What? What did I say? Is it that bad?"

My voice strained, trying to find the right words. "No, I'm okay. It's just my dad used to always say that to me. He'd tap me on my nose and ask me that question. It was always a little joke between us. I haven't heard anyone say that for a long time."

Collin wrapped me tightly in his arms. "I'm so sorry, Bailey, I didn't know."

"I know. It's okay, really. I'm fine. I was actually thinking of how this all feels like a dream for me. I've lived under a constant nightmare for so long, it's hard for me to really believe things could be right again.

Almost every night since the accident, I relive it in the nightmares, many times being woken up by my own screams. For the past couple of weeks, I've been able to sleep through the entire night, completely nightmare free. I can't tell you how amazing that is for me."

"You've had nightmares every night for the past two years?"

"Yeah, pretty much."

"And now they're gone?"

"Yes, because of you." Reaching up, I ran my fingers along the side of his face and down his cheeks. Our eyes locked, his blue eyes dark as the night; I felt like he could see into my soul. His arms tightened around me and pulled me closer to him; gently he touched his lips to mine. The tingling I always felt when we kissed raced through my body. My hands moved up behind his head, my fingers running through his thick hair. Slightly pulling back, he still kept me close, our faces just inches from each other, our noses touching, so slightly, so gently.

"I'm glad I could help chase away your nightmares."

"Me too."

"It's getting late, we should probably get back."

"Yeah, you're probably right, but I wish we could stay here, just like this, forever."

We walked back to the car loaded down with our bags and chairs. As we got closer, I could tell Savannah was maneuvering to get the front seat again. I vowed that she would be the one that ended up in the backseat on the way home. Dumping everything in the hatch, I was able to reach the passenger door first.

"Here, Savannah, go ahead and get in back. I'll hold the seat up for you."

Her eyes glinted with anger, which she quickly tried to hide, but it confirmed my fear that she could be potentially dangerous. Without a doubt, I knew that my instincts were correct and that I needed to watch her carefully.

Her voice was strained as she tried to sound normal. "Thanks, Bailey. I guess it's only fair that we trade off."

Smiling to myself, I knew it was petty, but one small victory felt good. I slid the seat back after she had climbed in and settled into the front seat with plenty of legroom.

The ride home was mostly quiet. It was late, and we were all tired from the day in the sand and sun. My hand lay interlocked with Collin's on the console most of the way home.

"I'm going to drop you off first, Savannah, then I'll take Bailey home."

"Oh. Isn't that kind of a waste of gas, though?"

"It's no big deal. The front door should be open for you. I'll be back in a bit."

The car stopped in front of Collin's house, and I opened the door and stepped out, allowing the front seat to slide forward so that Savannah could extract herself out of the tiny backseat. As she gracefully exited the car, our eyes caught. Her deep chocolate brown eyes were hard and cold, and hostility shot from them. The battle lines had been drawn, and we both knew it.

"Goodnight, Savannah, it was great meeting you." The lie stuck in my throat.

"You, too Bailey. I'm sure I'll see you again soon." Her voice was icy.

She turned and walked up the sidewalk with her bag, and I got back into the warmth of the car and to the boy that had stolen my heart.

~ *Savannah* ~

I had the urge to stomp all the way into the house. Fury blinded me; Bailey had no idea what she was up against. She might have the upper hand right now, but Collin was not something I had any intentions of losing. As I sat in that backseat all the way home, having to stare at their hands together on the console made me sick.

Earlier in the day I had seen Collin kissing Bailey, and it had made me crazy. Collin should be kissing me, not her. I didn't have very much time, and before long my family would be headed home, back to Las Vegas, hours away. I needed to get the ball rolling quick. Drastic times called for drastic measures. I just had to figure out what the best approach was going to be.

CHAPTER EIGHT

~ *Bailey* ~

The rest of the week was uneventful and seemed to fly by. I just had to make it through two more days until Savannah's family left town. That day couldn't come soon enough for me.

I rushed to finish getting ready, since I was supposed to be over at Eileen's in less than twenty minutes. It was taking me a while to get used to actually sleeping in the morning, and many times now, I had overslept my alarm. It was so good, feeling rested and alive. I felt like I was ready to take on the world again. The haziness of the past two years was quickly fading, as if I had finally left the shadow and moved into the sunlight, able to feel the warmth of life as it moved around me.

After grabbing the clothes I planned to wear that night on my date with Collin, I tossed them on the bed as I walked out the door. Time would be short after I was done babysitting Riley, and I would only have a few minutes to get ready before Collin would be there to pick me up. As I walked out of my room, I sent a text to him:

Bailey: morning babe :) have a great day I'll c u later
Collin: hey baby have fun with Riley text me when u r done and I'll come pick u up

Rushing down the stairs, I practically flattened my aunt as she was coming up.

"Sorry! I'm late for babysitting! I'll see you later."

"It's okay. Hey, Bailey."

Halting at the bottom stair, I turned to look back up at my aunt.

"Yeah?"

"It's good to have you back. I mean, really back. The shadows are gone from under your eyes, and you seem like yourself again. I can't tell you how happy it makes me."

Feeling the tears welling in my eyes, I took the couple of steps back up to my aunt and gave her a hug. Her face, so much like my mom's, yet different, had been a constant reminder of what I'd lost. At first that resemblance had been difficult for me, but I knew I'd never have been able to survive without her gentle care and unconditional love.

"Thanks, Aunt Rachelle. I love you, and thank you for being here for me."

Squeezing me harder, she whispered so softly, I could barely hear it: "I love you too." As I turned away, I could see a tear as it slid down her cheek.

~ *Savannah* ~

I walked through the McKenna house and noticed Collin's cell phone charging on the counter. I knew no one was around, and I stepped carefully to it, listening for anyone approaching. I quickly scanned the room to make sure I was alone, picking up the phone, I saw the text from Bailey. With only two nights left here, I was determined not to lose another night where Collin was out with Bailey. Glancing around to make sure I was still alone, I quickly sent a text to Bailey.

change in plans, not sure when I'll be free. I'll text u later

I didn't have to wait long until a message came back. I smiled as I read the reply:

ok just let me know

I deleted the last two texts and unplugged the charger from the wall, leaving the cord attached to the phone. Walking quickly away, I felt amazingly better.

~ *Collin* ~

I was sitting on the front porch swing with Savannah; we had been hanging out most of the day talking about old times. It was a nice change of pace. I'd always had a connection with Savannah, but for me it was just friendship. My mind drifted to some of the things Bailey had mentioned that day at the beach about Savannah wanting more than friendship from me. I was sure Bailey was just reading into things. Looking at Savannah, all I could see was my childhood friend, someone who was like a sister to me. Savannah would never be more than a friend; my heart belonged to another.

My mind was never far from Bailey, and I wondered why she hadn't texted me yet, but I brushed it off. I was sure Eileen must have been running late, but even then Bailey usually would let me know; this just wasn't like her. Absently, I felt Savannah's arm brush against mine. Her touch didn't scorch me like Bailey's did. I could feel my phone in my pocket and willed it to ring or signal a text.

I tried to focus on the story that Savannah was retelling. It was another one of our crazy adventures when we'd been kids. I had totally forgotten about this particular escapade. I laughed as I sifted details from my memory; we were always getting into some sort of trouble. I looked over at Savannah, and something in her gaze made me uneasy. In that instant, I felt that Bailey just might be right. There was a different sparkle in Savannah's eyes I'd never noticed before. Her cheeks were flushed a slight pink, and she had moved closer to me. I was usually more aware of girls' reactions, and I was kicking myself for not picking up on this sooner. I hadn't been paying enough attention, and now I realized Savannah's face was just inches from mine. She put her hand on my cheek and leaned in closer, her lips brushing mine. The kiss stirred no feeling in me; it was like I was kissing my sister. As I was pushing her away, I caught movement in the corner of my eye that made my heart sink.

~ *Bailey* ~

Pacing my room, I wondered why Collin wasn't returning my texts or calls. I had been home for over two hours now. Now that I thought about it, after this morning's texts, I hadn't heard from Collin all day. Since I'd been busy babysitting Riley, it wasn't unusual not to hear from him, but having him not return my calls or texts though was just weird. Picking up my phone, I dialed his number, but again it went to voice mail. Hanging up, I tossed the phone back onto the bed. I had already left two messages. A sickening fear washed through me and my heart started to beat faster. He could be hurt, or he could be with Savannah. Both of those options made me violently ill. It felt like my stomach had just shot up to my throat. I couldn't stay here any longer waiting, wondering. I grabbed my keys off the desk and decided I was going over to Collin's house.

The short drive seemed to take ages. My mind flipped through so many scenarios; none of them were good, and my imagination was running wild now. I pulled my car up to the curb, and there on the front porch swing were Collin and Savannah, sitting far too close for my comfort. Immediately the anger, and the feeling of betrayal, burned inside of me. My heart was beating so fast it felt like it would explode out of my chest. I sat there for a minute trying to understand how Collin could do this to me. Before I really knew what I was going to do, I was striding up the sidewalk, my anger stronger with every footstep. They seemed oblivious to my approach; Collin's back was to me, so he didn't see me. I reached the front yard just as they kissed. I could feel my arms shaking with a violence I had never felt before. I wanted to rip Savannah into tiny pieces.

"Sorry to interrupt. Guess if you'd had the decency to return my phone calls or texts I wouldn't be here to bother you," I spit out, the anger and hurt boiling inside of me.

Collin turned quickly toward me, shock evident on his face. He got up from the swing and was walking in my direction fast. "Bailey, wait. What are you talking about?"

"I've been home for over two hours waiting for you! I've called, I've texted, and you never responded."

"I never got any phone calls or texts."

"Yeah, whatever. I've seen enough. I'm not stupid. Go back to Savannah." The words ripped from me with raw anguish. I turned quickly and started running back to my car, the tears already burning my eyes.

Reaching the safety of my car, I jumped in and quickly drove away, tears now flooding down my face. Collin was just a blurry image on the sidewalk as I sped away. Sobs were racking my body, and I tried to calm them, brushing the tears aside so I could see out the front windshield. Trying to focus on the road, I drove through the streets not knowing where I was going, only that I wasn't going home. I needed to regroup, to think.

All that kept running through my head was why? Why would he lie about his feelings for Savannah? He should have just told me. It would have been hard and hurt badly, but at least it would have been honest. But the dragging it on, telling me that I was the only one, that he was falling for me, that's what hurt me to the core.

Before I realized where I was going, I found myself at our special lookout. I pulled over and just sat there, my hands still gripping the steering wheel. I bent over and rested my head against the cold hard plastic between my hands. The tears were flowing unstoppable now.

I don't know how long I sat there, my chest and my stomach aching from the crying. The haziness of the past two years was rapidly surrounding me. I could feel the numbness returning. How could I have been so dumb? Savannah and Collin had history, a lot of history, and she was so beautiful. Why wouldn't he want her? It only made sense. I would never be able to compare to her. I stared out the front window of my car; some far corner of my brain noticed the breeze picking up outside. My thoughts drifted back to the many times I had been here with Collin: our first kiss; the shooting star; sharing our fears and what we hoped our futures would bring. The memories only fueled a fresh round of tears.

~ *Collin* ~

I stood frozen on the sidewalk as Bailey's car sped away. I was still completely baffled. What was she talking about, not returning her calls or texts? I felt for my phone and removed it from my pocket. Was it on silent? Was it off? It was then that I realized that my battery was completely dead. Looking up from the phone, I saw that Bailey's car was already gone. Running to my Camaro, I jumped in and raced after her.

I drove by her house first, but her car wasn't out front. I wasn't sure where she was going, but since she wasn't home, I had a pretty good idea where I might find her. It would have been where I would have gone to find some quiet.

Driving to the edge of town, I turned onto the road that would take me to the lookout. I had driven this street so many times that I knew every twist, every turn, every bump like the back of my hand. Finally, the last turn brought her car in sight, and I could see her shadow in the driver's seat.

Pulling my car behind hers, I cut the engine, stepped out, and quickly covered the few steps to her car. I could see her shoulders shaking and knew she was crying. Watching her like this shattered my heart.

Quietly I opened the door and crouched down so that I was at her eye level. Opening the door startled her. Bailey's head turned, her usually light eyes dark and red-rimmed. Tears were still streaming down her cheeks. I couldn't stand to see her so upset—all I wanted to do was take her in my arms and hold her.

~ *Bailey* ~

The movement as my door opened scared me so badly, the scream got caught in my throat. I hadn't even heard another car approach, much less stop. I turned and was staring into the blue depths of Collin's eyes.

"Bailey, baby, please stop crying. Nothing was going on."

"Please, just leave me be. I know what I saw." My voice was shaky; I could barely get the words out.

"Really? What exactly did you see?"

"The two of you on the porch swing engrossed in each other and kissing."

"Bailey, we were sitting out there talking about old times, but that was it. She kissed me, it wasn't the other way around."

"But you still kissed her!"

"Yeah, my fault. I wasn't paying attention because I was thinking of you. I didn't realize until too late what she was intending. There was no feeling to it, baby. It was just a kiss like I'd give my sister."

"On the lips? You really kiss your sister on the lips? I highly doubt that!"

"No, I wouldn't kiss Lacey on the lips. What I meant was it didn't mean anything. It was like a handshake, okay? It's not like when I kiss you and I feel it burn all the way through me."

"I'm sorry, but kissing means more to me than something casual. Watching you kiss her killed me, like a knife being stuck into my back."

"Bailey, I'm sorry, okay? I didn't mean for that to happen. We were just sitting there talking. I was waiting for you to text me or call, wondering what was taking you so long."

Looking into his eyes, I felt like I was drowning and he was throwing me a lifeline. I ached to grab on and believe him. Could it really have all been as simple as that? His fingers gently wiped the tears from my face.

"You were waiting for me to call you? But I did, several times. I texted you too. Why didn't you ever answer them?"

He fished his phone out of his pocket and handed it to me.

"Battery is dead. I'm not sure how; I had it charging this morning. I was waiting for you. I was getting worried but just thought Eileen was working late."

I looked at his phone now clutched in my hand and flipped it open. It was dead, completely dead. Relief flooded me as all the pieces fell into place. Collin was not ignoring my phone calls or texts; it was all a huge misunderstanding. But I was not pleased about him kissing Savannah. The visual of that still stung, and I wasn't sure if I'd be able to get that horrible sight out of my head. His hands gently extracted mine from the steering wheel and pulled me out of the car. Once my feet hit the ground, he folded me tightly against his warm, strong chest. My head settled just above his heart. I could hear it beating strong and steady. Standing there in his embrace, the tears started again.

"I'm so...sssorry," I stuttered.

"Ssshh, it's okay, baby, it's okay." His hand stroked the top of my hair, brushing the tear-soaked strands away from my face.

Standing there in my own personal heaven, I was able to let go of my fear and the pain that had so utterly consumed me. I could feel him as he began to pull slowly away. His hands held my face firmly just a few inches from his, one hand on each of my cheeks. As I stared into his eyes, his gaze burned into my soul, melting me as I stood there. He leaned down to brush his lips against mine, lightly, tenderly, then deeper and stronger. I was lost in the tingling that flooded my body and shot through my limbs. Nothing mattered at this point but Collin. He pulled back gently, his hands still cradling the sides of my face.

"Bailey, I love you. You have completely invaded my soul and consumed my heart. I have never felt like this with anyone before."

"I love you too, Collin. Since the accident I have felt so broken and you've healed my heart. I thought it would be broken forever, but you brought the joy of every day back to my world. You've given me something to look forward to again."

My world had righted itself, and I leaned against Collin, relieved. I was a little ashamed that I had totally blown the whole situation out of proportion. Savannah's presence had severely undermined my confidence. I felt so plain next to her and couldn't wait until she was gone.

The laughter started then from deep inside me, a low rumble at first, then becoming full-blown hysterics. Collin looked warily at me, not sure what to make of this new turn of events.

"I'm sorry. Wow, I guess I acted like a crazy person, huh?"

Pulling me back against him, he chuckled a bit. "Well, maybe not a crazy person, but you sure scared the heck out of me."

He leaned down, grabbed my keys out of the ignition, and then closed the door. With his arms wrapped around me, we walked over to our bench and sat down, watching as the lights came on in the valley below.

It was late when he walked me back to my car, kissing me goodnight. I didn't want to leave him, but knew I needed to get home. I started my car and drove home under the blanket of stars.

A HEALING HEART

~ Savannah ~

Sitting on the porch swing, I enjoyed the interchange between Bailey and Collin. This was even better than what I'd hoped for. I never really thought Bailey would show up, but the timing couldn't have been better. I had just wanted to spend some one-on-one time with Collin, and with Bailey around, that wasn't going to happen. Trying not to smile, I watched as Bailey drove away, but when Collin raced after her, my heart sank. I really didn't understand how she could be so important to him! From what he'd told me, they'd only been going out for a few short weeks. It just didn't make any sense.

Several hours later, I was lying in the bed that I was sharing with my sister, unable to fall asleep. For what seemed like the hundredth time, I glanced at the clock's illuminated green numbers across the darkened room. One a.m., and still I hadn't heard Collin's car drive up. I could only hope that he hadn't found Bailey and that he was just out driving around. The thought of Collin finding her and making up drove me to madness. In an attempt to stay sane for the moment, I was not going to think in that direction.

Finally I heard the rumble of his car coming down the street. Bolting out of bed, I went downstairs wearing only my skimpy satin short pajamas and matching cami top. I had just reached the bottom of the stairs when Collin entered the house, shutting the door behind him. He looked up as he entered the house; he seemed a bit surprised I was standing there.

"Savannah." Collin's voice was cool, almost icy.

"Hey, Collin, I'm glad you're back okay. I'm sorry about Bailey. I can't believe she'd overreact like that."

I moved over to Collin and reached out to touch his arm in a comforting gesture. Collin shrugged my hand off of his arm, like he couldn't bear my touch. I was offended but tried to keep my temper under control.

"Savannah, you're a good friend; you always have been. We go way back, but let me be clear here. There is nothing going on between us. Not now, not ever, okay? You are like a sister to me, and that's all it will ever be."

I gasped but struggled to regain my composure and defuse the situation. I couldn't believe he was so angry. "Collin, I have no idea what you are talking about. Of course I know we are just friends. What makes you think I want us to be more than friends?"

"I'm leaving it at that. You know exactly what I'm talking about."

Collin brushed past me as he walked into the kitchen. I stood there in complete disbelief. It was not supposed to be happening like this. I wasn't giving up, though; I was just going to have to come up with a better plan.

~ *Collin* ~

Walking past Savannah, I was still upset with her games. I guess I couldn't blame her for trying. Next time, though, I'd be paying more attention and not get caught off guard. I mean, this was totally not typical for me. It was very troubling that one little slip of a girl could cause me to be so oblivious to everything else around me.

Placing my dead cell phone on the counter, I plugged it into the charger, but nothing happened.

"What the heck?" I mumbled to myself. As I tugged on the charger cord, the plug ended up in my hand. That was odd; I knew for sure this morning it had been plugged in.

Once my phone got some juice, Bailey's texts and voice mail messages came through. Reading through them and listening to her voice, I could almost feel her sense of urgency, as the texts got shorter and more abrupt. I was so sorry I had put her through that agony. All because of my damn phone battery. I'd learned one lesson, though. When my instincts were telling me something wasn't right, I needed to follow through. All it would have taken was for me to have picked up the phone and tried to call Bailey when I felt something was off. I would have known right then that my phone wasn't working. Electronics were great when they worked, but when they didn't, they sure could cause serious issues.

The next morning, the kitchen was full when I came down for breakfast.

"Morning, Collin, have a seat. I have something exciting to share with you and Lacey."

"What's up, Dad?"

"We're moving to Las Vegas right after your graduation."

"We're what? Dad, we can't leave now, we just got settled here. I like it here, Lacey likes it here. Why? Why now?"

"Shane offered me a great position at the company he's working at right now. The salary is fifteen percent more than what I'm getting right now and the benefits are better. Collin, I have to do this for our family. If you really don't want to go, you're eighteen now, you can choose to live on your own. I hope that's not what you choose, but it is your choice to make."

Lacey bolted from the couch where she had been sitting next to Ashley. She flung herself into my arms.

"Please don't leave me Collin, please." I stroked Lacey's hair tenderly, trying to soothe her.

"It's okay, Lacey, I won't leave you." My heart plummeted to my stomach. How was I ever going to tell Bailey? I realized that I wasn't going to be able to tell her, not yet, not until I had figured out some sort of plan. I needed some time to think things through first. There had to be a way to work it out. Las Vegas was not really that far away. Somehow, some way, we would make it work.

~ *Savannah* ~

I was sitting at the table across from Collin, trying really hard not to smile. I couldn't believe how easy it had been. I had given my dad just a few subtle suggestions on how great it would be if there was a job for Collin's dad. It would be like it used to be when our two families lived near each other again. Never in my wildest dreams did I think it would happen this quick. June. They'd be moving in June, just a mere two and a half months away. When Jared had given Collin the option to stay here, my heart had lurched, fearing my plan would backfire. But Lacey sealed the deal. I knew there was no way Collin would leave his beloved sister alone.

In just a little over two months, Collin would have to leave his precious Bailey and be miles away from her and just minutes away from me. Having Collin closer would give me a better opportunity to win him over. I knew in the end I would get him to fall in love with me. I just needed more time and Bailey out of the picture. Now to just wait out the next few months, and in the meantime, making a few plans wouldn't hurt.

CHAPTER NINE

~ Bailey ~

It had been almost four weeks since Savannah had gone home; I really hoped I would never have to endure her presence again. I was just extremely thankful that she lived a distance away.

April had quickly slipped by, and before I knew it, May had arrived, and with it my seventeenth birthday. Birthdays had always been something I looked forward to, before. Over the past couple of years, I had tried to ignore their existence. This year, though, I was actually a little excited; I wasn't quite sure what to expect. Collin had taken the afternoon off from work and was taking me somewhere after school. Later we were joining my friends for dinner at my favorite restaurant. I had tried several times to extract the details from Collin, but each time he refused to tell me what we were doing, simply saying, "You'll just have to wait and see."

I finished getting ready for school. I was wearing the new outfit my aunt and uncle had given me the night before. The deep green in the shirt made my eyes appear greener than their usual gray color, the jeans were comfortable, and I adored the tall brown leather boots that hit just below my knees. My aunt had a knack for picking out just the right thing for me.

When I reached the kitchen, my aunt was still sitting at the table with her ever-present coffee mug and a bagel while she read through the morning paper. As always, she was perfectly dressed in a pantsuit that set off her auburn hair and deep brown eyes, warm and tender just like my mom's. There were still times when it was unsettling that they were identical twins. It was comforting in some ways as it felt like my mom was still there with me; other times it was painful. Today it was just comforting.

"Morning."

"Happy birthday, Bailey! Wow, that outfit looks great on you! I knew it would bring out your eye color."

"Thanks, Aunt Rachelle, I love it! Thank you again." I reached the table and gave her a big hug.

"I'm glad. I have a special muffin for you. It's on the counter."

I glanced over to the counter and started laughing. Sitting on the counter was a blueberry muffin with candles covering the top. Without counting, I was pretty sure that somehow she had found room to shove in seventeen of them.

"I don't do the baking thing, and I know you don't really like the birthday cake or cupcake thing. You have always liked muffins, so I decided that was as good a substitute as any."

"Thanks. I guess there's always a first for everything, and I have to say that this is indeed my first birthday muffin."

My aunt got up from her chair and began lighting the candles.

"You really don't have to actually light them."

"Oh, yes, I do, and you're going to blow them all out and make a wish. It's the least I can do."

Laughing, I could not deny her. Once she had them all lit, I made my wish and proceeded to blow the candles out.

"There, now. It's officially your birthday. So, what did you wish for anyway?"

"Come on, now, you know I can't tell you, otherwise it won't come true!"

"Yeah, you're right, but I had to ask anyway. I think I can take a pretty good guess it has something to do with that amazing guy you've been seeing the last couple of months." She leaned casually against the counter, smiling.

The heat rushed into my cheeks, and I knew they were stained pink.

"Still not telling."

"I know, but had to try. You better hurry, though, so you're not late for school."

I finished my birthday muffin, grabbed my backpack, and walked out the door to my car. Once I stepped outside, I noticed there was something on my windshield. Locking the front door behind me, I hurried over to see what it was. As I got closer, I could see it was a long-stemmed red rose, with a note under it. I quickly picked it up and opened the note.

Happy Birthday Bailey!
I love you,
Collin

Grinning, warmth flooding through me, I wondered when he had come by. Usually I could hear his car approach, but this morning I hadn't heard anything. I tossed my backpack in the car and was off to school. The perfume from the rose was strong and my car quickly smelled like it was full of roses.

Mia and Natasha were waiting for me when I got to school, both greeting me with birthday wishes. I thanked them while scanning the crowd for Collin. He usually beat me to school, but today there was no sign of his car or him. It was getting late, so I went to English a bit disappointed.

Sliding into my seat just before the bell rang, I grabbed my notebook and was just setting my backpack on the floor when I could feel my phone buzzing. Grabbing it quickly before class started, I smiled. It was a text from Collin.

Collin: Sorry I missed u before class. Was running late. I'll see u in a bit. Love u!
Bailey: thanks for the rose! love u too

I slid my phone back into my backpack and focused on our morning assignment. Just before class ended, a student came into class and delivered a note to the teacher and left.

"Bailey, you have a message."

After pushing back my chair I walked to the front of the room and my teacher handed over the note. I opened it as I returned to my seat, reading as I walked, the note said I needed to go to the office. The bell rang, I grabbed my backpack and walked in the direction of the office, a little worried as to why I had to go.

Entering the waiting room of the office I noticed the huge arrangement of colored balloons with a large Happy Birthday balloon in the middle. My face turned beet red; somehow I knew they were intended for me.

"Are you Bailey?" the receptionist asked. I could never remember what her name was, but she was always smiling and nice.

"Yes."

"It seems you have a delivery."

Completely embarrassed, I walked across the waiting area to pick up the balloons. "Thanks." I took the arrangement and wondered what I was going to do with them the rest of the day; surely I wasn't supposed to carry them around with me. As I hurried out the door the balloons blew in front of me cutting down my line of sight so I never saw Collin's approach. I only felt his arms as they slid around my waist, pulling me tightly to him and turning me so that we faced each other.

"Happy birthday, babe!" His lips touched mine softly, making my legs feel like butter. It was still surprising to me how just his slight touch affected me so completely.

"Thanks. Don't you think the balloons are a little much?"

"Absolutely not. Now everyone will know it's your birthday."

"And that's a good thing?"

"Of course. Why wouldn't it be?"

"It's just a little embarrassing is all."

We started walking toward my next class, his hand holding my free one while my other hand held the obnoxious bouquet of balloons that trailed behind us.

Part of me wished I could just let them fly away, but the other part of me loved them because they were from Collin. Annoying or not, I would keep them.

"You look great, by the way. I love that shirt on you. It makes your eyes really bright."

"Thanks. It was a gift from my aunt and uncle."

"So are you ready for this afternoon?"

"Well, I would be if I knew what was up."

"You'll just have to wait and see."

His smile lit up his face, and I wondered even more about what he had planned for our afternoon.

I had raced home after school to freshen up a bit before Collin arrived to take me off to wherever he had planned for the afternoon. Checking the time, I realized I had a few minutes to spare and decided to use the curling iron on my hair. Just as I was finishing clipping a few strands back from my face, I heard Collin's car turn the corner down the street. I quickly spritzed my wrists with my favorite perfume and went downstairs to meet him.

The doorbell was ringing just as I reached the bottom stair. I threw open the door and was met not only by Collin but a tall glass vase full of what appeared to be not one but two dozen long-stemmed, red roses.

"Oh, wow! They're beautiful, Collin!"

"I thought you might like them."

"Thank you!" Taking the tall vase, I stretched up to give Collin a kiss and then walked toward the kitchen with him right behind me.

"So are you ready?"

"Yes. Are you going to tell me where we're going?"

"Nope, you'll just have to wait and see."

Laughing, I decided not to push the issue. It was actually kind of fun not to know what the plan was for the afternoon. After situating the vase on the counter, we went out to Collin's car. As we reached the passenger door, he stopped me.

"Do you trust me?"

"Um, yeeeesss. Why?"

"Okay, then turn around. I'm going to blindfold you so our destination is a surprise."

"Are you serious? I can't even see where we're going?"

"No, I told you it's a surprise. Are you game?"

"Sure, why not."

Collin reached around and carefully tied a silk blindfold over my eyes. "Can you see anything?"

"No. This better not make me carsick!"

"We're not going far, you'll be fine," he laughed.

Collin helped me into the car and buckled me in. I sat in darkness and focused on my other senses. Taking a deep breath, I could smell his cologne as it lingered in the car. I realized that the fragrance of his cologne would probably always fascinate me, its scent light and clean. It stirred a sense of excitement within me. Sitting in the seat, I racked my brain trying to figure out where he might take me. The driver's door opened, and Collin got in and started the car.

"Are you ready?"

"Yes, let's get this show on the road! I'm dying of curiosity now!"

The drive was pretty quick. I was trying to figure out where we were going, but after the second turn, I was totally disoriented. The car slowed and finally came to a stop.

"Can I take this off now?"

"No, not yet, just a little bit longer."

I heard Collin get out of the car and open my door to help me out. Holding my arm, he gently guided me along. The surface we were walking on was yielding, there were sounds of kids laughing in the background, and the smell of recently cut grass was strong. I realized that when my sight was taken away, my other senses seemed to take over. After a short walk, he stopped me and then helped me sit down. I could feel a soft blanket under my hands. The breeze had picked up and blew strands of hair across my face.

"All right, how much longer do I have to endure this?"

"Hold on, just a little longer."

I could hear clinking and something being shuffled around but was uncertain what he was doing. As I felt him move next to me, he finally untied the blindfold from my face. Opening my eyes, I realized we were in the park, the same park, under the same oak tree that he had been sitting under that first day we had "officially" met. A blanket had been spread for us to sit on, and in front of me was a picnic basket with snacks, sparkling apple cider, and a small silver-wrapped box. I was blown away; I couldn't believe he had gone to so much trouble.

"Happy birthday, Bailey!"

"Collin, this is crazy. I can't believe you did all of this! I've never had anyone do anything like this before."

"Well, do you like it?"

"Yes! What made you decide to do this here?"

"I thought our first meeting was special, an instant connection. I can't really explain it. I sat here under this tree watching you sitting over there on that bench, focused on Riley. There was something about you that drew me toward you. When our eyes met, it was like nothing I'd ever felt before. I knew I had to go over and talk to you."

"I felt it too, but you know, it really wasn't the first time we'd run into each other. The day before I about ran you over in the parking lot."

"Yeah, I remember. It's not every day a pretty girl comes flying into you."

"I didn't think you knew who I was. You didn't seem very happy."

"I knew who you were because of Quinn. I was in a hurry that day—my morning wasn't going well. Sorry if I was a bit abrupt with you." He flashed me his big smile and all I could do was laugh.

"I have to say, as of right now, I'm really not sorry I ran into you that morning. From that moment, things in my life have changed so quickly—for the better. I feel like my head is spinning."

"Yeah, I'm not sorry either, and I'm glad that I chose to take Lacey to the park that Saturday afternoon. It's like forces were moving beyond our control, tossing us into each other's paths." He picked up the small box that still sat undisturbed at my feet and set it in the palm of my hand. "Well, are you going to open this or not?"

"I think I'm being spoiled! First the single rose on my car, then the balloons, the two dozen roses, and now all of this? All I needed was you."

"You deserve this, Bailey, and I wanted to do this for you. So open it."

Taking the small silver box, I tugged the purple, glittered bow off the top and tore the paper. Lifting the lid of the box revealed a white leather jewelry box. I looked up at Collin in shock, wondering what could be inside the small box that I held in my hand. Carefully, I flipped the lid open to reveal a necklace. Gasping, I carefully lifted the pendant and watched it twirl in my fingers; it was a gold heart, with an emerald nestled in the center. Near the bottom of the heart on one side, there were two halves of a heart intertwined; each half had one small diamond set at the top. It was as if the two halves had melded together and formed the single complete heart. It could not have been more perfect. I could feel the tears forming in the corner of my eyes. As I looked up at Collin, the tears slid down my face.

"Collin, it's beautiful! I don't know what to say. I've never had anything like this."

"You like it? I thought it suited you. Here, do you want me to help you put it on?"

Removing the necklace from its box, I handed it to Collin and turned my back so that he could clasp it around my neck. After it was fastened, he turned me back around so that he could inspect it. "It looks good on you."

I reached up and held the necklace in my fingers; I was still in shock. "Emerald is my birthstone, but I'm guessing you already knew that."

"Yes. Do you know the history behind the emerald and the diamond?"

"No, I've never really thought about it. No one has ever given me jewelry like this before."

"I did a little research. The green of the emerald represents spring, or like starting over. They say that if you wear an emerald it brings wisdom, and patience and is also a symbol of love. In Greek society they believed that a diamond was a reflection of everlasting love. Some even said that diamonds were pieces of stars that had fallen to earth or were tears of the gods."

"I never knew there were such meanings for the different stones. That makes this gift even more special."

I shifted over closer to Collin so that I was sitting just in front of him, facing him. I leaned over to kiss his lips, my hands wrapped around his neck, my fingers threading through his thick hair. His hands came around my waist, pulling me closer to him; I was practically sitting on his lap. Slowly he leaned back a little, his nose gently touching mine.

"Thank you, I'll treasure it forever. There really are no words for how special this is."

"Good, I'm glad you like it. I think it was made just for you and was sitting there waiting for me to find it."

"So, I have to ask, how did you have all this set up here and be able to leave it to come pick me up?"

"Ahh...that's my secret. But I guess I will confess that I did have a little help holding down the fort while I went to get you."

Collin sat with his back against the trunk of the old oak. I was sitting in front of him leaning against his chest as we snacked on crackers and grapes. We had been sitting there for over an hour just enjoying being with each other when I noticed Eileen's car parking in the lot. Eileen got out, and after her bounded Riley and Lacey. Hand in hand, the two took off running. Riley, significantly shorter than Lacey, was trying hard to keep up with Lacey's longer strides. I knew they had seen us and were racing straight for us.

"Baiwey! Baiwey!" Riley called.

Collin got up and helped me up with him as we waited for them to reach us. Riley had let go of Lacey's hand and was headed straight into my arms. I grabbed him and swung him around.

"Hey, Riley, what are you doing here?"

"Came to see you! Happy birthday!"

"Ah…thanks, little guy!" I set him back down on the ground and tousled the top of his hair.

"Hi, Lacey. How are you?" Crouching down so I was at her eye level, I opened my arms and she came into them, a bit slower than Riley, but she gently hugged me nonetheless.

"Happy birthday, Bailey. We've got something for you."

"Really?"

Eileen had caught up by then. "Hey, Bailey, happy birthday! Collin invited us out here. He thought you would enjoy seeing the kids. They both made you cards, and they have been dying to bring them to you."

Turning I looked up into Collin's face, "What other tricks do you have up your sleeve for today?"

Chuckling, "You'll just have to wait and see."

With all of us sitting back down on the blanket, Riley crawled into my lap. "Here, open mine first!"

Taking the envelope from him that was colored with greens and blues, I opened it and pulled out his card. I could tell he had spent quite a bit of time coloring and drawing on it, but like most of his pictures, I would need him to explain to me exactly what he had drawn.

"See, here is you, and this is me, and this is a heart, cause I wuv you."

"It's beautiful, Riley, and I love you too." I reached down and hugged him tight, kissing him on his forehead. The little guy was very special to me.

Lacey quietly sat down next to me and handed me her card. I opened it to find two stick people inside: One was tall with short hair, the other was shorter with long hair. Their stick hands were touching, and they were standing inside a big pink heart.

"That's Collin and you."

"Thanks, Lacey, it's really sweet. I love it." It never amazed me anymore how observant little kids could be; they really didn't miss much.

Riley was the first one up. "Okay, can we play now?"

"Sure, you guys go play. We'll leave in a little bit."

Riley was gone in an instant, with Lacey not far behind, dashing to the play area.

"Those two are so cute together," Eileen commented.

"Thanks for having Lacey over with Riley today. She's really been looking forward to it."

"It was no trouble, Collin. They had a lot of fun together. Bailey, this is for you."

I took the card that Eileen handed me and opened it up. Inside was a hundred-dollar gift card for my favorite store.

"Thanks, Eileen! But it's really too much. You didn't need to do this."

"Bailey, you have been my lifesaver. I cannot tell you how much I've relied on you the past couple of years. It really is the least I can do. Go, enjoy, spend it on something you want."

I reached over and hugged her tight. What she didn't realize was that both she and Riley had been *my* lifesavers over the past couple of years. Babysitting Riley had gotten me through the endless days and helped me work through some of the loss of my family. They both had become incredibly important people in my life, and I was so thankful for both of them.

"That's a beautiful necklace, Bailey. I've never seen you wear that before."

"Thanks. I actually just got it. It was one of my birthday gifts from Collin."

"Well, I have to say that I approve. That's a really gorgeous piece of jewelry, Collin."

"Thanks. It was the first thing I saw in the case, and I knew it was meant for Bailey."

"You've got yourself a very special guy here; you better hold on to him."

"I know, and I will. Would you like some of our snacks?"

"Thanks, I'm good. We won't stay long. I promised the kids we'd go get pizza before I took Lacey home."

The three of us sat in comfortable silence watching as Riley and Lacey chased each other through the play equipment, laughing and giggling. Up and down, up and down, they never stopped. Where they got all their energy from I would never know. It seemed to be never-ending, until they just wore themselves out to the point of total exhaustion. Before long, Eileen got up, bade us farewell, and walked over to corral the kids. Both Riley and Lacey ran over for one last hug from Collin and me before they followed Eileen to the car and left.

"Well, are you ready for the next part of the evening?"

"Yes, where are we going now?"

"It's time to meet everyone for dinner."

Collin gathered up the blanket and picnic basket, and we walked back to the car. I couldn't wait to show Mia and Natasha my new necklace; I knew they would love it.

Dinner had been a lot of fun. My friends loved my necklace and told Collin he'd chosen really well. My seventeenth birthday had been more perfect than I'd ever imagined possible. I was indescribably happy, and I was cherishing every minute. Having spent the last few years in quiet misery, the happiness and excitement now were even more powerful. I was storing each memory, every feeling in my journal so that I could always go back and relive the emotions that I was experiencing right now. I didn't want to forget any of the little details.

I glanced over at Collin as he drove through the quiet streets. Our hands were intertwined together over the console. He must have felt my stare as he turned, his eyes catching mine, a grin spread across his face.

"What?" He asked.

"Nothing. Just looking at you."

"That's it?" He chuckled as he focused back on the road ahead.

"I like looking at you. You're pretty cute you know." I smiled at him as he looked back at me. He picked my hand up and lightly kissed the back of it before setting it back on the console.

A few more turns and we were parking up at the lookout. Collin popped the trunk as he slid out of the car and grabbed the blanket we had earlier at the park. The night was a little chilly as the wind had picked up. We walked hand in hand to our bench. I cuddled next to him, content. My head rested on his shoulder, his arm was wrapped around me, his fingers drifted up and down my arm.

With the blanket wrapped around us, we sat in silence for a while as the crickets chirped in the distance. The city lights twinkled below as far as we could see. I hadn't been this happy or content in a long time. I tilted my head back to look up at Collin.

"Thank you. I think this has been the best birthday ever."

"You're very welcome." He smiled as he leaned down, his lips touching mine.

The kiss intensified as he pulled me tighter to him, his warm tongue teased mine. I could taste the lingering chocolate from the cake at dinner. I could smell his cologne as I breathed in deeper. His fingers brushed lightly against the side of my breast, stirring an ache deep in the lower part of my stomach. I sighed as Collin broke the kiss, his forehead rested against mine.

"Baby, I don't think you know what you do to me." His eyes were intense as they searched mine. I felt a shiver run up my spine as I held his gaze. My arms had wrapped around him and lay open against his strong back. "It's very difficult to stop. I want you—more than anything."

My heart raced and my brain had turned to mush. What did I want? I had always thought I'd wait until I was ready to get married, but I never expected my feelings to be so strong at this age. Was I ready for the next step? I was torn. Would I lose Collin if I said I wanted to wait? I knew I loved him, without any doubt.

"Oh, Collin, I don't know what to say. I've never been with anyone before. I don't want to lose you, but I'm not sure I'm ready."

His fingers traced the side of my face. His deep blue eyes never broke contact with mine. "It's okay," he signed, "you aren't going to lose me. I promise. We can wait. I don't want to push you into something that you're not ready for."

"Have you been with someone before?" I asked, not sure I really wanted to hear the answer.

His eyes broke contact as he looked toward the valley before they returned to mine. In that instant I knew he had.

"Yes."

"Oh." I dropped my gaze to his chest. Watching it rise and fall as he breathed. My heart fell and then I panicked and I looked up quickly. "Was it Savannah?" I asked, my voice was barely a whisper.

"No, I told you we're just friends."

I sighed in relief. I could handle the one, but if it had been Savannah, I'm not sure I could have stomached that. Collin's fingers lightly touched my chin pulling it upwards. His eyes were intense.

"There's only been one. And to be honest, I never felt for her what I feel for you. I was in a really bad place after my mom left. There was a party one of my friends dragged me to, trying to get me out of my house. I just wanted to forget everything going on at home. Someone had gotten ahold of alcohol and everyone was drinking. I knew better, but I didn't care. I started talking to one of the girls in our class that I was friendly with. I didn't know her really well, but the attention she gave me that night, I craved. Before I knew it, we were up in one of the spare bedrooms. Afterwards, I regretted it, I still felt empty inside, even more so than I had. I promised myself I'd wait until I found true love." His fingers traced the side of my face. "I'll wait, Bailey. You are worth waiting for."

"I do love you, Collin. I promise you'll be the first to know." I grinned as he chuckled.

"I would hope so."

His lips took mine captive once again and I lost myself in the moment, savoring the time we spent together. After breaking contact, I leaned back against him as he held me tight, and we watched the stars fall from the sky.

CHAPTER TEN

~ *Collin* ~

The end of the school year and my graduation were rapidly approaching a mere two weeks away, with the imminent move to Las Vegas shortly after. I still hadn't been able to find the right time or way to tell Bailey about the move. I knew putting it off was only going to make things worse. I wished I knew what to do, how to tell her, or better yet, find a way to make the whole thing go away. The problem was that I knew that it wasn't going away and time was rapidly running out. Every day I wished that my dad would change his mind. I'd brought the topic up several times, but each time, my dad stood his ground and was determined that this was the best thing for our family.

My mind was racing with thoughts of Bailey as I maneuvered the Camaro through the wet streets and the thick fog that blanketed the city. During the night a storm had moved in; the smell of wet earth was strong. The air was cold and brisk, so unusual for the end of May. I was on my way to work. It was Saturday morning, and I was scheduled to open the store. Early mornings were actually one of my favorite shifts; it usually gave me more time to spend with Bailey in the afternoon.

When I was apart from Bailey, it felt as though my entire world was off kilter. My love for her ran deep, like nothing I'd ever felt for anyone before. It often frightened me, knowing how completely she had wound herself so tightly within my heart. Being with her was easy, comfortable, natural—just like breathing.

I was driving on autopilot, so engrossed in my thoughts my brain didn't even register that the car driving toward me was out of control. By the time the realization hit me, the other car was fishtailing on the slick, oil-covered road right in front of me. I swerved to the right in an attempt to miss it. Relief flooded through me as I thought I'd escaped when all of a sudden my car caught a slick portion of the road and the rear end came around, clipping the front passenger side of the other car. The impact sent my car spinning, abruptly halting as my side of the Camaro slammed into a streetlight, the metal crumpling and curving around the concrete post. My last conscious thought was that I had to be dreaming, this couldn't be happening. An image of Bailey's face flashed briefly before my eyes as everything went black.

~ *Bailey* ~

I woke up suddenly, my heart pounding; panic flooded my entire body, causing every muscle to shake. Sitting up, I glanced at the clock. It was only eight thirty a.m. I still had a little bit of time before I needed to get up and head over to babysit Riley. Taking deep breaths and trying to calm my racing heart, I tried to remember what I'd been dreaming about. It had been so long since I'd been awakened by nightmares, but I knew that this one was different. It was not the usual dream that taunted me. The vision was murky, and I couldn't make any sense out of what had frightened me so badly. Deciding that I should just get up and start getting ready, I dragged myself out of bed. I noticed I had a text message on my phone. Realizing it was from Collin made me smile and helped calm my nerves.

Morning babe, have a great day with Riley. I'll c u after work. Love u

I quickly answered back:

Love u too! Miss u!

I set my phone down and went into the bathroom. The steamy shower felt good. The hot stream pouring over my neck and shoulders released the last bit of tension still left in my body. Knowing I had been in there long enough, I sighed as I flipped the water off and grabbed my towel.

The weather had turned cold and was unusual for this time of year. The fog was so thick outside that I couldn't even see the house across the street. Grabbing jeans and a warm sweatshirt, I got dressed. After blow-drying my hair, I pinned it back away from my face so that it would be out of my way when I was playing with Riley. The house was quiet as I went downstairs for some breakfast.

Taking my bowl of cereal to the family room, I flipped on the TV. I searched through the multitude of channels looking for something interesting to catch my attention. The local news channel was full of reports of the weather, with news anchors cautioning those on the roads to be careful. A story on a recent accident was starting and I flipped the channel quickly to avoid seeing the wreckage. I propped my feet up on the ottoman and finished my breakfast while watching cartoons. Before long, it was time for me to leave.

My car was cold, and I waited patiently for the heat to kick on. As I drove toward Eileen's and approached the downtown area, I noticed the flashing lights of police cars and fire trucks. A tow truck was pulling what appeared to be a mangled green Dodge up onto its flatbed. Accident sites always made my stomach jump up into my throat. I hoped that no one was seriously hurt. Turning left, I continued on my way.

Riley was watching for me in the front window, his face pressed against the cold glass. As soon as he saw my car, I could see his arms waving frantically, and then he disappeared. I reached the front door and knocked on it, knowing that Riley was waiting on the other side.

"Hello? Is anyone home? I'm looking for a little boy. His name is Riley."

I could hear giggling on the other side of the door, but no response.

"Uh-oh, I guess he's not home."

The door flew open to reveal Riley's little face, so excited, grinning from ear to ear. Eileen stood just behind him. "I'm right here, Baiwey!"

"Ah...so you are. I need a big hug from my little man!" I stepped into the house and scooped him up in my arms, his body squirming.

"Good morning," Eileen greeted me as she shut the door behind us.

"Morning. I see Riley is full of energy today."

"When is he *not* full of energy?" she laughed.

"Yeah, you're right. Hey, there's an accident down on Main Street, and they have the whole thing blocked off. You might want to go around on your way to work this morning."

"I hope it wasn't anything serious. This weather sure is weird. Usually it's blazing hot and we're running the air conditioner."

"I know, but I have to say I'm not complaining. I prefer the cooler weather."

"Very true. We'll have hot weather soon enough."

Eileen finished getting ready and left for work. Riley and I settled into our normal routine; we colored, and played with his cars and trucks. After a while we cuddled on the couch watching one of his favorite movies. It was almost over when the doorbell rang. Shifting Riley off my lap, I went to the front door. I was a little shocked when I found that it was my aunt standing on the other side. Opening the door, I let her in.

"Hey, what brings you over here?" My throat got tight as I could see the tension radiating from her face.

"Bailey, sweetheart, I think you need to sit down."

"Why? What's wrong?"

I stumbled to the nearby couch. Riley had run in and jumped up in my lap, his head nestled against my shoulder.

"Honey, it's Collin."

I became very still as I felt the room begin spinning out of control around me. Riley's arms around my neck were the only thing grounding me. I stuttered to get the words out of my mouth. "What about Collin? What happened?"

"There was an accident this morning on his way to work."

My mind quickly shot back to the image I had seen with my own eyes just a few hours ago: the flashing lights, the wrecked car—but only one car. I hadn't seen Collin's car.

"No, there must be a mistake. The car was green; I saw it. It wasn't Collin's."

"Bailey, Collin's in the hospital. His dad called the house a few minutes ago looking for you."

"No, no. It's not possible." The words were barely audible as they slipped from my lips. My head swam with images of my family, but this time it was Collin I saw lying there lifeless. The grayness was quickly engulfing me. I tried to push it back. I needed to know he was okay.

"Bailey, it looks like he's going to be all right. But he's suffered a concussion, and he's unconscious. As of right now, his left leg is broken and a couple of ribs are cracked. The only thing that saved his life was the airbag. His car hit a light pole on the driver's side. They had to extract him out using the Jaws of Life."

Trying to focus on the words and their meanings, I held on to the first thing she had said. "But he's going to be okay?"

"Everything looks okay right now. He's young; he should heal. I already called Eileen and told her. I'll take both you and Riley to the hospital, and I'll watch Riley until Eileen is off."

I sat there still in disbelief. This could not be happening—I couldn't go through this again. Collin had to be okay; there just was no other option. Going through the motions, I grabbed my backpack and keys. With my aunt's help, I got Riley's bag put together and we left the house.

The ride to the hospital seemed like it took forever. I stared numbly out the window, not really seeing anything. By the time we arrived, I could barely focus, and everything seemed tinged with a gray haze. A little voice in the back of my head kept telling me I had to pull myself together.

I held Riley's small hand in mine as we walked silently into the hospital with my aunt. At the front desk we were directed to the Intensive Care Unit waiting room. Turning the corner, I caught a glimpse of Lacey, tears streaking her cheeks; the sight stabbed at my heart. I knew firsthand what she was going through. She looked up, as we entered the room. She jumped down from her dad's lap and fell into in my open arms. I scooped her up and held her tight.

"Bailey, I'm so scared."

I tried to get the words to come out of my mouth. I had to be strong for her. "Hey, it's going to be okay. Collin is strong, he's going to be just fine." I was surprised at how steady the words sounded because my legs felt like they had turned to Jell-O and dizziness overwhelmed me.

Lacey's tears soaked through my sweatshirt where her head lay. My aunt had made her way across the room to Jared, and they seemed to be introducing themselves. It looked like Jared was giving her an update. I watched the emotions flicker across my aunt's face as she took in what was being said. I set Lacey back on her feet, and Riley immediately grabbed Lacey's hand and hugged her. He didn't understand what was going on, but he knew that his friend was sad and he was trying to comfort her. It simply brought more tears to my eyes.

I walked over to where my aunt and Jared stood. I had only met Collin's dad a couple of times. He had always been polite and cordial, but somehow distant. Today I could see the anguish and raw emotion on his face and knew that however distant he might seem, the love for his children was strong.

"Hi, Bailey. The doctor says he's going to be okay; he's a little bruised up and has a few broken bones. They're not sure how long he'll be unconscious, though. He seems to have hit his head pretty hard on the side of the car when it impacted."

"What happened? I saw part of the accident aftermath, but didn't see Collin's car, just a green one."

"The other driver was conscious and was the one to call in the accident. He told the police that he'd lost control of his car and was headed toward the oncoming traffic. Collin had tried to veer out of the way but didn't quite clear the car. The back end got clipped, causing it to spin out of control. It was just pure bad luck that the light pole was right at that spot."

I closed my eyes, trying not to picture Collin's car wrapped around the light pole, but the image was already burned into my brain. My aunt's arm had found its way across my shoulder; she pulled me tightly against her. I could feel the light kiss on the top of my head. Her words were almost a whisper.

"Bailey, it's going to be okay. You have to believe that."

"They are only letting family in right now, but I'll get you in somehow, okay?" With that, Jared turned and walked toward the nurses' station.

I found my way back to Lacey and Riley as they sat quietly next to each other, their little hands entwined. The tears seemed to have stopped momentarily for Lacey, but her blue eyes were streaked with red. Sitting down next to her, I felt her lean up against me.

"I'm so glad you're here, Bailey."

"Me too."

We sat there in silence; I had no words for her. The panic that I'd been trying to push away was rapidly overwhelming me. I knew if I succumbed to it, I would be no help to anyone. Lacey and especially Collin needed me right now. A shadow fell across my legs, and I realized that Jared had come back and was standing with his hand outstretched in front of me.

"If you want to sit with him awhile, I'll take you in."

I nodded in silence.

"They're keeping the visiting down to short intervals for now."

"Okay."

I followed him through the double doors and down a corridor. We stopped at a room, and he stepped aside while I fought the anxiety inside me. Taking those final steps into the room where Collin was laying was one of the most difficult things I'd ever done.

A HEALING HEART

"The nurse will come get you when it's time to leave and bring you back to the waiting room."

"Okay. Thanks, Mr. McKenna."

"Call me Jared, please, you don't need to be so formal."

Jared turned and walked back in the direction we had come from. I nodded and took a few more steps into the room. Memories of Brooke flashed through my mind, and I remembered hoping that I would never see another ICU again. Light flooded in from the window. The curtain around the bed was only partially shut. I took a deep breath; the smell of antiseptic assailed my nostrils. The beeping from the monitors was constant, the fluorescent lights were dimmed. An IV drip was set up at the head of the bed with its tube connected to Collin's arm. I finally gathered enough courage to look at him lying so still in the bed.

His face was pale, his beautiful blue eyes closed, a bandage wrapped around his head; there were cuts on his cheek. He had a pretty big gash above his left eye where I noticed they had stitched it closed. His left leg was bound in a cast. I could see his chest was wrapped, the rest of his shoulders and arms bare where the sheet didn't cover. I could feel the tears streaming down my face as I tried to stifle the sobs that threatened to burst from me.

I found my way over to the bedside, standing on his right side. I carefully leaned over and kissed his warm forehead. Sitting down on the chair next to the bed, I linked my fingers through his and sat there silently crying, wishing this was all just one of my horrible nightmares and that I would wake up soon.

"Collin, you can't do this to me, I can't go through this again. Please wake up," I pleaded with him.

Lifting his hand to my lips, I kissed it gently, then held it against my cheek, silently willing his fingers to move, his eyes to flicker open. I closed my eyes as the tears continued to slip down my cheeks.

"You're going to be okay, but you've got to open your eyes. Please. I love you."

I sat there with my head leaned over his hand that I held tightly in mine. The light touch on my shoulder startled me.

"Miss, he needs his rest. You'll need to step out for a while."

"Okay, sorry."

I swiped the tears from my eyes and reluctantly let go of Collin's hand. I stood up and leaned over, kissing him lightly on the lips and whispering to him how much I loved him.

The nurse standing there waiting for me was younger than I had first thought, small and pretty, her hair clipped back from her face. There was compassion in her deep brown eyes. "There's no reason why he isn't going to make a full recovery. He just needs to rest. I'll let you know when you can come back in and sit with him again."

"Thank you." I turned to leave the room, looking back at Collin as I got to the door. The view of him in the white bed made every bone in my body ache. Turning away, I left the room, my footsteps silent on the shiny floor as I walked back to the waiting room.

A HEALING HEART

~ *Collin* ~

My body felt heavy, everything felt sore, and I couldn't get my brain to function right. I wasn't even sure where I was. The last thing I remembered was being on my way to work and thinking about Bailey. My throat felt like it was full of cotton balls; a strange murkiness seemed to engulf me. I could hear people talking, but their words were mumbled and quiet and I couldn't make any sense of them. I was so confused. I tried to open my eyes, but they wouldn't open. It was like my body wouldn't listen to my brain.

It was quiet, but I felt an electrical charge race through my body. Something touched my forehead, just slightly, tenderly. I knew instantly it was Bailey. I knew she was here with me, and I needed to tell her I was okay, that I loved her, but the words wouldn't come out. I could hear her talking, pleading for me to wake up.

My hand was warm as she held it. I tried to squeeze her fingers, but nothing happened. I silently cursed my body for not responding. The effort to make my body move drained what little energy I had. I was so tired, and I slipped back into the darkness.

~ *Bailey* ~

My aunt was waiting for me when I got back to the waiting room. She immediately got up from her chair and walked over to me, folding me into her warm embrace. I stood there within her comforting arms and quietly cried. I needed to pull myself together. It would not help Lacey if she saw me so completely out of control. When I finally got hold of myself the best I could, I backed away, breaking the embrace, but my aunt did not let go of me. Her arm was still tightly around my shoulders as she guided me to a chair. I noticed that Jared was talking with what must be Collin's doctor. He was nodding, and I saw him shake hands with the doctor and then return to sit beside Lacey and quietly talk to her.

"I can't leave, Aunt Rachelle. I have to stay here for now."

"I know; it's okay. I'll take Riley to our house until Eileen gets off. I already called Mia and Natasha. They're both on their way over here to be with you."

My aunt stood up and walked over to where Riley and Lacey sat. Jared got up from his chair and the two of them talked for a minute. He nodded and then my aunt crouched down in front of Lacey.

"Hey, Lacey, I'm Bailey's aunt. I'm going to take Riley to my house for a while. Would you like to come over and play with him?"

Lacey's eyes darted to her dad's and he nodded his head in assurance that it was okay. Lacey simply nodded yes. Her hand still clutched Riley's. The two little kids hopped off their chairs. Riley hurried over to me and flung his arms around my neck. I held him tightly, soaking up his unconditional love. I set him back down on his feet, and Lacey was in my arms next.

"It's going to be okay, Lacey. I'll stay here with Collin, okay?"

Nodding, her face filled with pain and worry, she grabbed Riley's hand, holding it like her life depended on the connection between the two of them. I sat back down on the chair and watched my aunt leave with the two little ones. Jared came over to sit next to me, awkwardly patting my shoulder.

Uncertain how long we sat there in silence, my mind drifted through so many memories, both good ones and those that were pure agony. I was so absorbed in my memories that I didn't even notice when Mia and Natasha walked in until they were right in front of me. I looked up at both of them, and a new flood of tears came pouring out. They both held me tightly, reassuring me that everything was going to be okay. Jared had gotten up and was pacing the waiting area. It was then that I noticed that Quinn had come with them; he was talking with Jared across the room from us. The young nurse that had ushered me out of Collin's room entered the waiting room and stopped to speak with Jared. I watched the interchange intently. After a few minutes, Jared gestured to me, and the nurse walked in my direction.

"Bailey?" she asked.

"Yes."

"You can come back again if you wish."

"Thank you."

Mia grabbed my hand, "It's going to be okay, Bailey. We'll go get you some coffee and be right back."

Nodding gratefully to them, I turned and followed the nurse. Walking down the hall toward Collin's room, the need to be with him was overpowering, but at the same time, an unsettling apprehensiveness settled over me. Reaching his room, the nurse stepped aside as I entered. I sat back down in the same chair I had occupied just a short time earlier.

Grasping Collin's right hand in mine, I sat there watching his unmoving body. His eyes were still closed;

his beautiful features almost frozen in time. He looked so peaceful. The constant beeping of the machines around him seemed to fade. The only thing I could focus on was this boy, who had come to mean more to me than anything else. I had to be positive, to really believe deep down inside me that he was going to be okay. But I had been down that path before, and the pragmatic side of me warned that things don't always turn out the way I may want.

"Hey, Collin, I'm back. I'm here, waiting for you. I know you can wake up. You've got graduation in just two weeks, and you can't miss that. Just squeeze my hand, let me know if you can hear me."

I waited intently, watching every breath he took, waiting for any muscle to move, but there was no movement.

"I love you so much, my heart hurts."

Still nothing. I wasn't going to give up. I sat there until the nurse came in and said it was time to go.

I leaned over and kissed him, telling him that I would be back soon. Back in the waiting area, Mia and Natasha were waiting for me with coffee as they had promised. I sat down next to Mia as she handed over the cup.

"Thanks."

Jared had taken a seat across the room. He was leaned over with his head in his hands, my heart went out to him.

I took a drink of the coffee in my hands. It was hot; I didn't even notice the flavor much, I just knew that it warmed the inside of me.

The day crept by, with no change in Collin's condition. He was stable, and that was a good thing, we were told over and over. Through the day, Jared and I took turns sitting with Collin. Quinn went back once; when he returned to the waiting room, his face was stark white. I knew seeing his friend in that condition in the bed had been difficult. The next time he was asked if he wanted to see Collin, he said he would just stay in the waiting room as support.

Mia and Natasha had dragged me down to the cafeteria for some food, but I couldn't taste any of it. I mostly pushed it around on my plate and just needed to get back up to Collin. I was afraid that something would change and that I wouldn't be there.

When we came back up to the waiting room from the cafeteria, my aunt was there with Lacey, who was sitting in Jared's lap with her face buried in his shoulder. My aunt got up from her seat and walked toward us.

"He's going to be fine, Bailey, he just needs to rest. His body went through a lot today."

"I know, I keep telling myself the same thing."

Jared, with Lacey in his arms, came over to us then.

"I need to get Lacey home and ready for bed. They're going to call me if there's any change. I'll be back here first thing in the morning. I'll call you, Bailey, if I hear anything."

"Thanks, but I want to stay here."

"Bailey, you need to get home and get some rest too. You aren't going to be doing Collin any favors if you get yourself sick," Jared replied.

"I can't leave, I just can't. I won't be able to sleep even if I do leave."

"Bailey, please, you do need to rest. I'll take you home," my aunt insisted, siding with Jared.

With the decision being out of my hands, I was forced to leave the hospital with my aunt. She dropped me off at Eileen's to pick up my car, and it took all my self-control not to immediately drive back to the hospital. As it was, I knew that I'd be up first thing in the morning and back with Collin.

I tossed and turned all night, unable to sleep. When the early morning light began streaming in my window, I threw back the tangled sheets and dashed through getting ready so that I could get back to the hospital.

In the kitchen, I grabbed a granola bar out of the pantry and tossed it into my purse in case I might need it later. Leaving a note on the kitchen table since both my aunt and uncle were still sleeping, I quietly left the house.

The hospital parking lot was virtually empty this early in the morning. I found a space quickly and proceeded into the building with dread. I hadn't heard anything last night from Jared, so I assumed that there had been no change through the night. I crossed the quiet and almost-empty lobby, the cleaning staff moving efficiently through the area preparing for the day, and I followed the maze of hallways to the ICU.

The ICU waiting room had a cluster of people in one corner, anxiously hugging and talking among themselves. Though I was preoccupied, I mustered a brief positive thought for them. I hoped they would have good news soon. Walking past them, I found the nurses' station and asked about Collin's condition. The nurse in charge of Collin's care was a different one from the day before, and she politely but firmly informed me that if I wasn't immediate family, she couldn't give me any information. Frustrated, I turned and went back to the waiting room to wait until Jared arrived.

A TV hanging from the ceiling in a corner of the room had an old rerun on it. Strangely, I hadn't even noticed it was there yesterday. I'd brought the book I was reading with me today and flipped to where I had left off, but I couldn't focus on the story. After rereading the same page for at least the third time, I tossed it back into my purse.

Slowly the minutes ticked by. The show that had been on the TV was over and a new one was starting. My eyes sought out the clock mounted on the wall; it was now seven a.m. Where was Jared? I hoped he would get here soon so that I could find out what was going on.

The room was a bit chilly this morning, and I wrapped my sweatshirt tighter around me. I wished now that I'd taken the time to drive through Starbucks and get a coffee; the stuff here in the hospital wasn't very good.

With nothing to do now but wait, I began watching the group of people in the corner. A young lady, in maybe her mid-thirties, was sitting in a chair. I could tell she was in the late stages of pregnancy. Her blond hair was in a ponytail, and her face was frighteningly pale. An older lady with graying hair at her temples was sitting next to her—their features were so similar that they had to be related—the younger woman's hands in her own. The other three, all men, were standing clustered together speaking quietly.

The door to the waiting room opened, and a doctor approached the group. He spoke to them for a while, put his hand on the pregnant lady's shoulder, smiled and nodded. From across the room, I could see apparent relief in her face and the tension release from her shoulders. The group's mood immediately improved as the doctor turned and slipped out of the room. It appeared that their news was good, and I was happy for them. So many times, the news in hospitals was only bad; at least this once it was nice to see the opposite. Now, if only Collin would wake up. It wasn't long after that Jared appeared at my side.

"Hi, Bailey. You're here bright and early."

"I know; I couldn't sleep. They wouldn't tell me anything when I got here, though, since I'm not immediate family."

"Okay, let me go get an update. When I called in last night, there had been no changes."

Jared left my side and vanished through the double doors to the nurses' station just down the hall. He wasn't gone long. When he returned, I couldn't read the expression on his face. Was it good news or bad? I couldn't tell.

"Everything's the same. I did ask them to allow you to go in and visit. They said you could go back for a short time."

"No, you go first. You're his dad; it's only right that you see him."

"I see now why my son seems to be so drawn to you. You have a good heart."

With that, he turned and left the room. I'm not sure what I expected him to say, but it wasn't anything along those lines. I knew it must be very difficult for him to see his son in the hospital and feel totally unable to do anything. It was a feeling that I had known all too well. Jared wasn't gone long, and I was surprised when, after only a few minutes, he was back in the waiting room.

"I didn't want to use up all his visiting time. I know you've been here for a while, so go back and spend the rest of the time with him."

"Thank you!"

I grabbed my purse and hurried down the corridor that would lead me to Collin.

His room was still fairly dark; a small light glowed just over his bed. With his window not facing east, it was still in shadow this early in the morning. He looked the same as yesterday, except I noticed his face now had dark stubble over it, giving him a more rugged appearance. I approached his bed after setting my purse on the counter and took his right hand again in my own. I leaned over, gently brushing my lips against his warm forehead. He felt a bit flushed, like he might be running a slight temperature.

I sat in silence, watching his rhythmic breathing and the dripping of the IV as it flowed to his arm, hearing the constant beeping of the machines, and begged him to open his eyes, to come back to me. Too soon, the nurse came in and ushered me out, promising to let me return. Giving Collin one last longing look, I picked up my purse where I had left it and returned to the waiting room. This waiting, the unknown—it was driving me to madness.

Arriving back at the waiting room, I was greeted by both Mia and Natasha. They were the best friends anyone could ever hope for. Natasha held a cup of Starbucks coffee for me, which just increased my appreciation for them tenfold.

"You guys really didn't need to come this morning."

"Yeah, right. We're not leaving you here alone," Mia replied.

"Here, we picked this up for you, knowing you probably wouldn't do it yourself and that you'd need it."

"Thanks! I can't tell you how bad I was craving that earlier." I accepted the warm cup from Natasha and drank my favorite blend.

"Any change?" Mia asked

"No, not yet. Still the same."

"Well, that's not bad news."

"I know, it's just I'm impatient. I want him to wake up. This waiting around is driving me crazy."

"And if I know Collin, I'm sure it's driving him crazy too. You know, they say that even though a person is unconscious they can still hear people talking to them."

"I know, and I hope he can hear me."

"I'm sure he can, and when his body is ready, he'll wake up."

The three of us sat there in comfortable silence. The routine of the day was established: I would go back when the nurse would let me. My friends would drag me off to get something to eat when needed. Jared came and went; Quinn stopped by and stayed for a while, refusing, though, to go back into Collin's room.

A HEALING HEART

Before I realized how late it had gotten, the sun was setting and there was a pink glow cast through the waiting room windows. I'd always enjoyed the setting of the sun more than the sunrise. Maybe because I'd always been more of an evening/nighttime kind of person and I didn't enjoy the early morning hours as much.

I walked back into Collin's room for what would probably be the last time today. My aunt had already called me to let me know in no uncertain terms that I needed to come home soon, or she would come to the hospital and drag me out of here herself. I had no doubt that she would do just that. Finals were just around the corner, and I had to get ready for them. I wondered what the school would do for Collin, since his graduation day was so close.

Taking my place by his bedside, I sat there holding his hand and looked out the window toward the mountains in the distance. My mind was drifting when I felt his fingers moving in my hand. My eyes flew back to search Collin's face.

"Collin? Collin, can you hear me?"

This time, the squeeze was harder, and I knew I hadn't just imagined it.

"Collin, I'm here for you. You're going to be just fine."

The grip relaxed but then tightened again. The beeping of the machines started accelerating slightly. I watched his face intently for any sign of movement. Then his eyelids began to flutter a bit, and finally they opened, and I could see the crystal blue of his eyes.

"Bailey." Just the one word, so quiet, barely audible, brought the tears back to my eyes and they streamed down my cheeks.

"Oh, Collin. I've been waiting for you to wake up. You had us all so scared."

"What...What happened?"

"You were in a car accident; your car ended up wrapped around a light pole. Your dad has been worried sick, Lacey too."

His eyes closed, and I worried he had slipped away again.

"Collin? Collin, can you still hear me?"

"Yes, I'm just so tired. Everything hurts. I remember now, the car was headed straight for me. I swerved; I thought I'd cleared it. I don't remember anything after that."

"They said the back of your car clipped the other car, sent you into a spin and around the pole. Your airbag probably saved your life."

"I'm sorry."

"Sorry? Why are you sorry?"

"For putting you through this. I'm so sorry."

"It's not your fault. Everything is going to be fine now. You're back with me. I'm okay; I'm complete now. Just please don't do anything like this again. I'm not sure my heart can handle it."

"I love you, Bailey."

"I love you too, Collin. I need to go get a nurse and let them know you're awake and to let your dad know too."

"Don't go, not yet. Please, just sit here for a minute."

"Okay. Whatever you want."

"I could hear you talking to me. Everything was fuzzy. My mind was telling my eyes to open, my body to move, but it wasn't listening. It was very frustrating for me."

"It's okay. I'm just so happy you're awake."

"Yeah, me too."

I got up and leaned over to kiss him. This time he was able to return my kiss, his lips dry but gentle. His right hand touched the side of my face.

"Thank you."

"No, thank you, for returning to me, Collin."

"I'll never leave you. I'll always be here for you."

"You better! Now, I really need to go get the nurse and your dad. I promise I will be back."

"Okay."

I walked out of Collin's room with a lighter step. I informed the nurse that he was awake, and then I proceeded to the waiting room to give everyone the good news. A huge weight was lifted off my shoulders; all would be well.

CHAPTER ELEVEN

~ *Bailey* ~

Collin had only spent a couple of days at the hospital after the accident and was released, the cast on his left leg a constant reminder of that horrible morning. He still wore the bandages around his ribs, although the pain from them being cracked was slowly going away. I knew firsthand how badly cracked ribs could hurt. All things considered, he was mending quickly, and I was thankful. Since Collin's car had been declared completely totaled, I had taken up chauffeuring him around, and it was a task I enjoyed. I knew, though, that he missed his Camaro and had been on the lookout for a replacement. My little Cobalt just didn't cut it.

Finals were over and I could say goodbye to my junior year. After graduation tonight, I'd officially be a senior, and I was really looking forward to the following year.

It was Collin's graduation day, and today was going to be a hot one. It was early morning and already the temperatures were climbing into the nineties. The sun was bright and intense as it beat down, a huge contrast from just a few short weeks ago. Thankfully, the graduation ceremony was in the late afternoon, so maybe the temperatures would cool a bit.

Collin had asked if I'd pick him up before graduation. He'd forewarned me that the Porter family had arrived from Las Vegas and would be in town for a few days. Having Savannah back in town made my skin crawl, but I bit back any comment and was hoping for the best. So far, I had yet to run into her, and the longer I could put that off, the better.

I sat at my desk, finishing the graduation present I was making for Collin. It was a scrapbook full of photos of us from the past couple of months. I was finishing the notes and detail work. Flipping through the pictures made me smile. It had taken me a long time to figure out what to give him for graduation; I wanted it to be something special and I hoped he'd like it. Reworking the note at the end for probably the hundredth time, I finally finished it.

My dearest Collin,

Words cannot express to you how happy you've made me. You have brightened my life and helped pull me out of the darkness that I was living in. Just one look from you makes me melt, and your tender touch and embrace complete me. You mean more to me than I ever thought possible. These photos are memories of the time we have spent together, and I hope that we have

many more to come. I love you with all
that I am.
– All my love, Bailey

Deciding the book was complete, I carefully
wrapped it up, finishing it off with a ribbon. I was never
one for the standard stick-on bows and always used real
ribbon. The gift bags so common these days were nice
when you were in a hurry, but never looked as pretty.
Setting the gift back down on the desk, I went to my
closet and removed the outfit I would wear tonight.

Mia, Natasha, and I had spent several hours at
the mall looking for the perfect dress. I'd come across
an ivory, halter-top sundress that skimmed just below
my knees. The dress had faint emerald green pin
striping. The wide belt around the waist was a deep
emerald green. I had found ivory ballet flats that were
comfortable, matched perfectly, and completed the
outfit.

The afternoon flew by, and before long, it was
time for me to get ready. I curled my long hair and
fastened small sections allowing, the soft ringlets to
taper down my back. Applying my makeup, I accented
my eyes, glad that I no longer had deep shadows under
them. It was amazing what a good night's sleep could do
for a person. I misted my neck and wrists with my
favorite perfume and left the bathroom.

Reaching my dresser where my jewelry box sat
on top, I opened it and pulled out the necklace that
Collin had given me. I wore it every day, only taking it
off at night. It was such a special gift—I knew that I
would treasure it forever. Sifting through the section
that held my earrings, I found the pair of emerald and

diamond studs that had once belonged to my mom. I had never worn them before; the painful memories had always been too intense. My dad had given them to my mom as an anniversary present the year before they had been killed. Today, as I fastened them in my ears, they felt right. It was amazing how well they matched the necklace—almost like they were a complete set. It was as if my mom was there with me, nodding in approval. I knew she would be happy that I was wearing her jewelry instead of letting them sit unworn.

Tucking Collin's gift safely under my arm, I left my room and glided downstairs and outside. The second I started my car, I turned the air conditioning up full blast. The heat outside was stifling, and I hoped it would begin to cool off soon. It already felt like my makeup was melting off. I sent a quick text to Collin letting him know I was on my way.

Collin was coming out the front door, his deep green gown slung over his arm, the cap dangling in his fingers, just as I pulled up. He was wearing an ivory long-sleeve shirt that was rolled up just above his elbows, a tie that had greens and browns swirled through it, and khaki dress slacks. The cast on his leg was almost entirely concealed. His hair was slightly tousled with gel. When he smiled as he walked toward me, it sent shivers down my spine. Every time I was with Collin the energy between us was intense. It still amazed me that out of all the girls in our school, I was the one Collin had chosen.

The passenger door opened and Collin gracefully slid in, an amazing feat since one of his legs was bound in a cast. He laid his cap and gown on his lap and shut the door. Before buckling his seatbelt, he leaned over to kiss me.

"Hi, baby. I've missed you. You look amazing."

The heat quickly flashed to my cheeks. It was still hard for me to accept the compliments he lavished on me all the time.

"Thanks. You look incredibly handsome yourself."

"Well, let's get this show on the road. My family will be on their way to the stadium shortly. You can sit with them if you'd like."

"It's okay. Mia and I are going to sit with Natasha's family. Natasha is already there and saving us a spot."

"You know, Savannah has been on her best behavior since they arrived. You don't need to worry about her, okay? She's already apologized to me about a hundred times for what happened during spring break. She's just a friend and that's it."

Forcing a smile, I turned to look at Collin. "Okay." It didn't relieve the awful sensation I had in the pit of my stomach every time her name came up. I still didn't trust her.

We arrived at the stadium and I had to circle around a couple of times to find a parking spot. Getting out of the car, we were blasted by the severe heat. The asphalt parking lot intensified the heat waves, and it felt like we were walking through an oven. I was glad that at least it was a dry heat and not dripping with humidity. Collin grasped my hand in his as we walked toward where the rest of the senior class was gathering.

Quinn found us first, his gown unzipped and the golden tassel on his cap bouncing as he walked toward us.

"Hey, buddy, glad you finally got here!" Quinn gave Collin a good-natured slap on the shoulder.

"Hey, Quinn. Let's get this over so we can go have the real fun after."

"Yeah, no kidding, I hear the party after is supposed to be crazy."

Collin handed me his cap while he slid his gown on and zipped it up. Setting his cap on his head, I helped adjust it.

"Hey, Quinn, can you take a picture of Collin and me?"

"Sure."

I handed over my phone that I had tucked in my purse and leaned against Collin. His arm wrapped around my waist, and he pulled me against his side. After snapping a couple of pictures, Quinn handed back my phone.

"Thanks, Quinn! I better go find Natasha and Mia. I'll see you both when this is over."

Turning, I found myself in Collin's warm embrace and being kissed soundly.

"I love you, Bailey." His grin lit up his eyes so they sparkled mischievously. One look from him could completely undo me.

"I love you, too." Totally embarrassed since Quinn was standing right there, I said goodbye to Collin and went inside the stadium, knowing my cheeks were bright red.

~ Savannah ~

Standing in the bedroom window on the second floor of the McKenna house, I pushed aside the gauzy white curtains and peered down at Collin as he walked toward Bailey's car. I had learned a valuable lesson the last time I was here, and I would not be repeating the same mistake. During the past months, I had hoped that, when my family returned for Collin's graduation, Bailey would no longer be in the picture, but that didn't seem to be the case. It was incredibly frustrating.

Knowing that Collin's family would be moving to Las Vegas in just a few weeks, though, was a huge step in the right direction. Surely Collin would forget about Bailey after a while, and I would be there waiting. Smiling, I turned to finish getting ready for the graduation ceremony. Patience...I just needed to be patient. I would have the one thing I desired most: Collin. I'd always gotten what I wanted, and this would be no different.

~ Bailey ~

The graduation ceremony had moved quickly through the speeches and award presentations but bogged down during the tedious process of reading the names of five hundred-plus graduating seniors. Finally, it was over, and we were trying to thread our way through the thick crowd and reach the group of seniors before they could all scatter. I caught sight of Collin standing under a tree. Lacey was wrapped in his arms, and she was laughing. It made my heart catch; he was so tender and loving with her, and she was such an important part of his life. It made me love him that much more, if that was even humanly possible.

As Mia and I reached Collin's side, I caught sight of Savannah standing next to Jared. I pasted a smile on my face and nodded to her.

"Hello, Savannah."

"Hi, Bailey."

Her response was almost as forced as mine, but I could feel the strength of Collin's arm as it wrapped around my shoulder, holding me tightly against him. With that reassurance, my jealousy and uneasiness slipped away. I turned my attention back to him.

"Collin, I'm so proud of you! I have a little graduation present for you, but it's in the car."

"I can't wait to see it."

Savannah's parents, Shane and Lynette, had reached the group now and were congratulating Collin. They told Collin how proud they were of him and that it was hard to believe he had grown up right under their noses. Before long, our little group grew when Quinn's family joined us. Natasha walked over to Mia and I as we stood at the edge of the group.

Laughter and hugs were passed around. Everyone was trying to figure out where they were going for a celebration dinner. I noticed that Savannah had slid closer to where we were standing. Quinn was standing next to her, and they were chatting about Las Vegas and the heat. I could make out most of what they were saying. I was curious but, at the same time, trying not to pay much attention to Savannah. I figured the less I focused on her, the saner I could stay. She got under my skin, and I didn't like her one bit.

I was crouched down talking to Lacey when I sensed Savannah and Quinn's slight movement toward us as Savannah was chatting away. Something wasn't right, and I stood up to focus on what was being said.

"Yeah, didn't you know? They're moving in a couple of weeks," I heard Savannah say to Quinn.

"Moving? Who's moving?" The questions slipped from my lips before I could fully digest what Savannah was saying. I saw Quinn's expression, and I felt a shiver of fear chase down my spine. I knew in my heart I didn't want the answer to the questions I had just asked.

"Collin's family. Oh my, didn't you know? They're moving to Las Vegas. My dad got Jared a job with his company," Savannah explained in a tone just dripping with sweet innocence.

I felt like I was going to faint. I knew the color left my face when Quinn took a step closer to me. I turned to face Collin, my sweet Collin. It couldn't be true; it had to be another lie from Savannah. Collin would have told me. I looked deep into his eyes and saw the hurt in them and knew in that instant it was the truth.

"Collin? Is it true?" My words were barely a whisper.

His eyes closed as he took a deep breath. "Yes. I just didn't know how to tell you. I wanted to so many times, but it was never the right moment."

My safe world that I knew deep down couldn't last was indeed shattering around me, just as I had feared that it would. Tears were forming in my eyes, and I brushed them back before they could spill down my face.

"How long have you known?"

"Awhile."

"How long?"

"Since the end of spring break, right before Savannah's family left."

"Spring break?" the words squeaked out. "That was over two months ago. When exactly were you going to say something? Or were you just going to leave?" The anger was starting to fester, burning deep inside me.

"Bailey, come on. Let's go talk about this."

"No. You've had plenty of time to tell me and you didn't. I trusted you, I believed in you, and you couldn't tell me this? You let me go on thinking you would be there. You lied to me."

"Bailey, it's not how it seems."

"No? Then why? Why keep this from me?" I could see everyone in our group watching us. Natasha and Mia were at my side; I felt Natasha's arm on my shoulder.

"Come on, let's go talk. I'll explain everything."

"No."

I was losing control, and I knew it. Not wanting to be the center of attention any longer, I extracted myself from Collin's restraining hand. Immediately, I felt as if I had been ripped in two, like a piece of me was left behind. Turning away, I ran for my car, swerving in and out of all the happy people around me. I could barely see them: the tears streaming down my face turned them all into a blur of color. Mia and Natasha were calling for me, asking me to stop, but I couldn't; I had to get to my car and get out of here. Collin's voice was mixed in there as well, but his broken leg slowed him down. I knew I only had a slight head start.

Finally reaching my car, I unlocked the door and slid in. My eyes caught on Collin's gift sitting on the seat almost as if it was taunting me. The sobs were tearing through my body as I raced out of the parking lot. Mia, Natasha, and Collin were just mere specks in the rearview mirror.

The pain cut so deeply into my heart and soul, I trembled. I felt out of control, spinning, uncertain of which way was up. How could he have kept this from me for so long? When was he going to tell me? It made me doubt and question everything. What other things had he kept from me, shielded from me? We could have prepared, made plans, worked things out. Now I wondered, was it all real? Somehow I'd known deep down things were just too good to be true. As much as I wanted the entire fairy tale, the happy ending, I knew it was just that—a fairy tale, and fairy tales didn't come true in real life. I had gotten swept up in the thrill, the excitement, and thinking maybe, just maybe, fairy tales could come true, but I was wrong.

I drove around aimlessly for a couple of hours, just thinking. The sun was setting and bright pinks and oranges tinged the sky, but I could barely see the colors or the beauty. It was as if everything was shaded in that old familiar washed-out gray color, like the light in my life had just been snuffed out—again.

Finding myself back at my aunt and uncle's house, I decided it was probably best if I went inside to my room. I needed to just be alone. Picking up Collin's gift off of the passenger seat, I walked quietly inside. As I entered the hallway, I ran into my aunt.

"Bailey, are you okay? Collin's been by here twice and called almost every fifteen minutes worried about you, saying you aren't answering your cell. What happened?"

"It's nothing."

"Nothing? Come on, honey, I can see with my own eyes this isn't 'nothing.' You look horrible, you have mascara streaked all the way down your face, and your eyes are red. What is going on?"

"Nothing."

I turned and ran up the stairs into my room, slamming the door shut. I tossed the present on my desk and flung myself on my bed, burying my head in the pillows. I let myself really cry now, the tears streaming freely, with what was left of my mascara streaking my pillowcase. I wasn't alone for long. I never heard the door open or shut, but I felt the bed as it shifted under my aunt's weight. She sat down beside me, quietly stroking my back.

"Honey, please tell me what's wrong. This is breaking my heart."

"Collin's m-m-m-mo-oving," I stammered out.

"Oh, Bailey, I'm sorry. It can't be that bad. Where's he moving to?"

"Las Vegas."

"That's not very far away. You guys can still talk and see each other."

"No. He lied to me. He's known since spring break and he never told me. Savannah lives in Vegas— he's going to be living near Savannah. I was just someone to hang out with. It was all just fun and games. He never had any other intentions, so that's why he never said anything."

"Come on, Bailey. Do you really believe that? So it wasn't cool that he didn't tell you, but do you really believe he felt nothing? That the past few months have been just fun and games? And who's Savannah?"

"He says she's just an old family friend. But she wants to be more than that. I'm not stupid, I could see it all over her face the first time we met. Her family was here during spring break."

"Bailey, I really think you're overreacting. If he didn't feel anything for you, then why is he so worried about you right now? Why won't you talk to him?"

"Because I can't. It hurts too badly. He's leaving in a couple of weeks, Aunt Rachelle. When was he going to tell me? As he drove off?"

"Honey, I'm sure he had his reasons. Why won't you at least let him try to explain?"

"I can't. I should have known better. But I thought maybe, just maybe, something good in my life could happen."

"You can't always think everything bad is going to happen to you. Good things do happen too."

"Please, I just need to be alone for right now."

"Okay. But I'm here if you want to talk about it."

She leaned over, kissed my forehead, and left the room, closing the door behind her. I was left in the deafening silence. A few minutes later, I could hear the phone ringing in the other room. I tugged the pillow around my head and tried to ignore it. My cell phone was still in my purse. It had been on vibrate during the graduation ceremony. I had never turned the sound back on, and I had no intention of turning it back on now.

A HEALING HEART

~ Collin ~

I stood there in stunned silence as Bailey turned from me and began running through the thick crowd. The hurt in her eyes pierced me to the core. I'd known the day was coming when I would have to tell her, but this was not how I'd wanted to do it. Cursing, I knew I had to go after her, talk to her, make her understand.

Mia and Natasha were already chasing her, but my damn cast slowed me down. If it wasn't for this broken leg, I could have easily caught her. I reached the parking lot just in time to see Bailey's car exiting the driveway. Mia and Natasha stood at the curb, and they both turned on me.

"Good going! What the heck is going on, Collin?" Natasha was practically screaming. "How could you keep something like that from her? She's been through enough, she doesn't need this! Does Quinn know?"

"Look, I know that. I just couldn't tell her. I didn't know how. Every time I tried, something came up. I didn't want to hurt her. I was trying to figure out a plan before I let her know, and I kept hoping my dad would change his mind. Sometimes he'd decide we were going to move and then something would come up and we would stay put. I didn't want to put her through all of this and then we never end up moving. I know it's not an excuse, but I was clinging to anything. And yes I told Quinn but asked him not to say anything until I had told Bailey."

"Well, that's just stupid. You guys never think. She's stronger than she believes, but this is going to crush her in a way I can't even imagine. You didn't see her or know her when she first moved down here. I did.

I saw how lifeless she was, barely moving from day to day. Then you come into her life, and I see a spark I'd never seen before. She deserved that, she deserves happiness; right now when she ran off, I could see that spark was gone. Her eyes were dull and lifeless again. That fast, in a split second, you stripped from her the hope that things in her life could be normal. Just because you had to lie to her. Didn't you learn anything about her over the past few months?" Mia's voice was almost as loud as Natasha's was as the words cut through my heart. I knew that everything she said was true.

"Yes, I did. Which is why I didn't want to tell her; I didn't want to cause her needless pain."

"Yeah, well that sure backfired. The damage is done now. What are you going to do?" Mia asked, her voice softening slightly.

"I don't know. I need to talk to her."

"Good luck with that. You need to decide what you are going to do. You either let her go now and let her heal, or you fix this. Don't be playing with her emotions." Natasha stated.

"I have no intentions of letting her go. I need to borrow someone's car and go find her."

"Here, take mine. You're not a bad guy, Collin, but I swear, you better make things right. My car is over there."

Mia yanked her keys out and handed them over as she pointed to the far edge of the parking lot.

"Thanks, Mia. I always knew you liked me."

Grinning, I grabbed the keys from her and hobbled toward the car as quickly as I could. Grabbing my cell phone I dialed Bailey's number, after several rings it went to voice mail. "Bailey, please call me back. We need to talk."

Finding Mia's car, I got in, sliding the seat back to accommodate my long legs. I was thankful the car was not a stick shift. I drove over to Bailey's house first, but her car wasn't out front. My next stop was the lookout where I'd been lucky to find her before when she had been upset, but again, there was no car there. Though I carefully searched the streets as I drove through town, I never came across her. I drove to the park, but it was empty. I was quickly running out of ideas. Where could she have gone? I continued to call and text her cell phone, as well as her house phone, but nothing. I was beginning to worry. Twice I stopped by her house, ringing the doorbell and talking to her aunt, but she still hadn't shown up there. I called Natasha and Mia, but neither of them had heard from her. Bailey wasn't taking their calls either. It had been over two hours now. I decided to try her house number one more time; her aunt picked it up on the second ring.

"Hello."

"Rachelle? It's Collin again. Have you heard from Bailey?"

"Yes. She's home now."

Relief flooded through me; at least she was safe.

"Thank goodness. Can I talk to her?"

"I don't think she'll take the phone, Collin. She's really upset."

"I understand. But I need to explain, to let her know what is going on."

"What *is* going on, Collin? Why would you lie to her about moving?"

"So she told you."

"A little."

"It's not that I didn't want to tell her, I just never knew how to, or every time I tried, something came up. I didn't want to hurt her. She means more to me than anything. I just need to talk to her."

"I believe you. I'll tell you what. If you come over here, I'll let you in. I know she'll be pretty mad at me, but I think she needs to hear the words from you."

"Thank you! I'll be right there."

I turned the car around and sped toward Bailey's house. Her car was parked out front. After parking Mia's car I hobbled out and up to the front door. Bailey's aunt was waiting and opened it to let me in. She never said a word as I followed her upstairs where she opened Bailey's door and stepped aside for me to enter.

Bailey lay on the covers, her face buried in the pillows, her shoulders shaking silently. Every once in a while she would take a deep shuddering breath and it ripped my heart out watching her in so much pain. Pain that I had caused; I wanted to be able to take it away, to make it all better.

"Please, leave me alone."

"Bailey, please. I'm so, so sorry."

She flipped over immediately, her face registering complete shock, like cold water had just been poured over her. Her face was white as a sheet, black streaks down her cheeks, her eyes red and puffy. I felt like I'd just been punched in the gut; looking at the girl I loved in such pain crushed me. As the door shut behind me, I carefully made my way to the edge of the bed and sat down.

~ *Bailey* ~

Collin's voice startled me. How did he get in here? I had thought it was my aunt returning. Flipping over on the bed, I stared at him as he sat down on the edge of my bed. Wanting it to be real, wanting him there but then thinking it had to be just a dream. I felt horrible, my body ached, my eyes burned—I knew I was a mess.

"Bailey, please stop crying. I'm sorry, so sorry I didn't tell you earlier. I just never knew how to tell you. I kept hoping that my dad would change his mind."

"But you leave in a couple of weeks, Collin. When were you going to tell me?"

"I really don't know. Soon. I didn't want to hurt you."

"Guess that didn't work out, did it?"

"Baby, please. I'm sorry. I feel bad enough as it is. My dad gave me the option of staying here, but I can't leave Lacey. She begged me not to leave her. She's only four, she still needs me. Las Vegas isn't too far, and I promise to visit all the time. We'll figure something out. I just wanted to have a plan before I said anything to you. I also hoped, really hoped we wouldn't move, that I could talk my dad into staying here."

His deep blue eyes pleaded with me. I could see the anguish deep inside their clear depths, and I was drowning. I knew he couldn't leave Lacey, and I would never ask him to do that. But I needed him too. Collin had given me a new hope that I could be happy again, a new outlook on life. How would I get through the days without seeing his smiling face, feeling his touch? Though the hurt lingered, my anger was melting. I couldn't understand how with just a few words, his presence, and just one look, he could so easily wipe all rational thought from my head. Sitting up on the bed, I brushed away the wetness from my cheeks, black staining my hand.

"Oh, Collin, you can't leave me. I need you too."

Collin reached over and pulled me against his chest. The warmth that radiated from him comforted me. His hand stroked my hair as he rocked me like a child, whispering soothing words. Closing my eyes, I just let him hold me, my arms wrapped tightly around him, thinking that maybe, if I held on tightly enough, I could keep him here. But I knew deep down that I would have to let him go; a part of me wasn't sure I would be able to.

"It's all going to be fine, Bailey. I'm not going to leave you. We'll figure something out. I promise. I love you, and I'm not letting you go."

With my face still buried in his shoulder, I cried until I had no more tears left.

CHAPTER TWELVE

~ *Bailey* ~

Bright sunlight was beginning to stream through my window. It was the morning after Collin's graduation. Rolling over in bed, I realized I was exhausted, uncertain if I had really even slept at all. My clock read five a.m. It had been months since I had been awake this early. It felt as if all my energy had been sucked out. Curling up into a ball, I squeezed my eyes shut, willing myself to go back to sleep. But I knew it was hopeless; there was no way I was going to be able to fall asleep again.

Collin had stayed late the night before. My aunt had allowed us to remain upstairs as long as we kept the door open. Most of the time he just held me, kissing me softly on my forehead. Words had failed me; I was still in shock that in just a few weeks Collin would be a couple hundred miles away. Just the thought brought another fresh batch of tears to my eyes.

I felt bad he had missed his entire graduation party looking for me. The guilt of taking away that special moment from him was intense. I had been looking forward to the party as well, but the bitterness of being kept in the dark about his moving away was still so strong.

I wished he had told me earlier, given me a little more time to adjust to the idea. Maybe then graduation would have been the happy event that it should have been. I would have had a chance to prepare mentally. I wondered, though, if I was just fooling myself. If he had told me earlier, would things really be any different right at this moment? Deep down, I knew the answer was no. All that really happened was that I had lived the last few months in a bubble of happiness where reality didn't exist. If he had told me earlier, I would have just felt the pain I was feeling now sooner. It didn't change the fact that he was still moving. But in the end, after thinking things through, I couldn't be mad at him for not telling me. It had hurt me and shattered my heart, but ultimately, it was the fear of losing him that stripped me to the bone, blinding me to all other rational thought.

The excitement that I had previously for the upcoming summer was gone. I only felt emptiness now. The light that had guided me out of the darkness I had been living in was all but extinguished, and I would have to move forward again by myself. Collin had promised he would call all the time and come visit as much as he could. I believed he would do his best, but eventually, I knew things would come up and he wouldn't be able to make that drive every weekend. It was too much to ask of him, and I loved him too much to expect it.

My head told me everything would be okay, that we would somehow make it work. I only had my senior year to finish. After I graduated, I could go to college wherever he was next summer, but a year felt like an eternity. My heart ached and I doubted everything. The conflict in my head and heart battled and I wasn't sure which one would win. I knew I was an emotional wreck, and I didn't know how to even start putting myself back together.

Accepting that there was no way I was going to get any more sleep, I groaned and rolled out of bed. As I walked across my room, my present for Collin caught my eye. There it was, sitting on the desk in its bright and pretty wrapping, a glaring reminder of what had once been. Looking at it now caused new tears to blur my vision as I entered the bathroom.

The face that greeted me in the mirror was a stranger. My eyes were red and puffy, the dark circles were starting to reappear, my face was white as a sheet. Turning away from the reflection, I turned on the hot water, stepped under the soothing spray, and tried to wash away the heartache.

Grabbing a pair of gray sweat shorts and a black T-shirt, I got dressed. After brushing out my tangled hair, I left it down to air dry. I just didn't have the energy to blow-dry it this morning. Downstairs, I found both my aunt and uncle sitting at the kitchen table eating breakfast and drinking their coffee.

"Oh, honey, you don't look so good," my aunt said as she pushed back her chair and walked toward me.

Plastering a fake smile on my face, I attempted to be positive. "I'll be okay. It's not the worst thing that can happen to me, right?"

"Bailey, honey. I'm so sorry."

She gathered me in her arms and held me tightly. I was trying to keep the tears pushed back; I had cried far too many of them in the last twelve hours. Pulling away, she kept her arm across my shoulder and steered me to the kitchen table.

"Here, sit. Let me get you some breakfast."

"I'm really not hungry. I could use some coffee though, if you have any left. I didn't sleep well last night."

"You need to eat something. How about a piece of toast with your coffee?"

"Okay."

Winning a battle against my aunt was impossible. It was easier just to give in. She placed a mug of coffee on the table for me—well, it was mostly coffee. I always drowned it with creamer, but it still had caffeine in it, and that was what I needed this morning. She went across the kitchen, grabbed two slices of bread, and dropped them in the toaster. Watching her quietly as she moved, I sipped the coffee she had given me. There was no way I was going to be able to eat both pieces of toast. The thought of food right now made my stomach turn. My aunt pulled out the apricot preserves and margarine from the refrigerator and slathered them both over the toast. After finishing her task, she set the plate with the toast in front of me.

"Thanks."

"You're welcome."

She returned to her seat next to my uncle, her eyes never straying from me. I didn't want to be a burden to them. They'd given me so much in the last two years. For my aunt's sake, I took a couple of bites of the toast in front of me. If I hadn't seen her put the apricot preserves on the bread, I'm not sure I would've even known that it was there. The bread seemed to grow in my mouth, completely flavorless. Washing it down with the coffee, I continued to progress through the first piece and take a couple of bites of the second piece before I gave up. Hoping that would be enough to satisfy my aunt, I pushed my plate aside and finished the coffee in silence.

My aunt and uncle chatted about their activities for the day, trying to draw me into their conversation and inviting me out, but I declined. I was in no mood to venture out of the house today. After rinsing my dishes and sliding them into the dishwasher, I went to the family room to watch some TV.

Curling up in the corner of the couch, I flipped through the channels but found nothing in particular that drew my attention. Just as I was starting some mindless movie, the doorbell rang. I glanced up at the clock; who would be coming over this early in the morning? Assuming it was probably just a salesman, I ignored it. When the doorbell rang again my aunt went to the door to investigate. Hearing voices but nothing specific, I focused back on the TV.

Looking up, expecting my aunt to be the one to come around the corner, I was a bit surprised to find Collin standing there; he was so handsome, my heart skipped. Without a thought, I bolted off the couch and threw myself into his arms. This was where I belonged, but I knew our time would come to an end soon, and I didn't know what the future held for us.

"Morning, baby." His breath stirred the hair on the top of my head as he held me close.

"Morning. What are you doing here so early? I thought you were supposed to be at breakfast with your family and the Porters."

"I was, but being with you is more important right now."

"Your dad wasn't mad?"

"He was a little, but he understood."

I couldn't make myself let go of him, clinging to him like my life depended on it. With a little difficulty, he maneuvered us toward the couch and sat down, pulling me into his lap sideways. Wrapping my arms around his neck, I just sat there with my head on his chest, over his heart where I could feel it beating strongly. His shirt smelled faintly of his cologne.

"You don't look like you slept much."

"No, I didn't."

"Nightmares again?"

I just shrugged.

"Bailey, I'm so sorry. It'll be okay. I promise."

"I'll live. I'm a survivor. Isn't that what you keep telling me?"

"Yes. You're one of the strongest people I know. We can make this work. Technology today is amazing, and I'll only be a couple hours' drive away. It's not like I'm headed clear across the country."

"I know, but it'll still feel like it."

Tilting my head up, I looked deeply into his concerned eyes. His fingers brushed aside the damp hair from my face.

"I love you, Bailey. You mean everything to me."

"I love you too, Collin. It's just going to be such a lonely summer now."

"I promise to come visit as much as I can, and you can come see me too."

"I'll have to work on my aunt and uncle—I'm not sure they'll let me drive that far."

"Well, we'll figure something out."

"I'm sorry you missed your graduation party."

"It's okay, I didn't miss much. It's no big deal."

"Speaking of graduation. I still have your present. It's upstairs—I'll go grab it."

Climbing out of Collin's lap, I went to get his present. As I went up the stairs, I noticed my aunt and uncle had vanished. I'd been so focused on Collin that I hadn't even noticed they'd left the kitchen. After picking up the colorfully wrapped gift from my desk, I returned to the family room where Collin waited. I took my place next to him on the sofa, one of my legs crossed underneath me as I sat sideways facing him and handed him the package.

"I hope you like it."

Taking the package carefully from me, he began to untie the ribbon. "I know I will because it came from you."

"I didn't really know what to get you. I figured you could use a new car, but that was a little out of my price range."

That made him laugh. "Yes, I could use a new car. I think I've found one, by the way. It's another Camaro, the same year I had before; this one is burgundy, though, instead of white."

"Yeah, I guess you better hurry up and get a new one, since you're going to be spending a lot of time on the road," I said, trying to keep my tone light and teasing.

Collin ripped the paper off the album. The cover had a picture of us standing in front of the castle at Disneyland; it was one of my favorites, a constant reminder of how everything had felt like a fairy tale for me. Carefully, Collin began flipping through the album. Pictures from our Disneyland trip, the park with Lacey and Riley, our trip to the beach, and my birthday were interspersed with random shots from school. I sat there quietly, watching the expressions flicker across his face. When he reached the last page and the note I had written, I saw his eyes get watery. It was one of the few times I'd ever seen him get teary eyed. He was usually so in control of his emotions.

"Thank you, babe, I think this is one of the best gifts ever."

He set down the album and leaned over, his hands resting on the sides of my face as he pulled me to him. His lips took possession of mine, at first kissing them gently but building in intensity. As always, I immediately responded to his touch with tingling throughout my body and butterflies fluttering through my stomach. My hands wrapped around his neck, tangling in his hair. Our emotions were spinning out of control fast when he pulled back, breathless. I didn't want him to stop.

We spent the day together, just us, with me snuggled against Collin's side. We were content to just be with each other, even if it was only watching TV. I pushed all thoughts of his leaving out of my mind; I would deal with it later. Right now I was focused on spending every minute I could with Collin over the next couple of weeks.

A HEALING HEART

The day I'd been dreading had arrived. Sleep had evaded me throughout the night, and I knew my eyes would be red because they were already burning. I had spent every minute I could with Collin during the past couple of weeks. Sitting in his room helping him pack, though, had been one of the hardest things I'd ever done. The boxes made it all more real, and I just wanted it all to go away.

Collin's family would be leaving on their journey after lunch. I wanted to get over there as quickly as I could this morning so that I could spend every minute possible with him. Knowing it was a waste to put much makeup on, I rushed to get ready. After putting my hair in a ponytail and getting dressed in jean shorts, a blue T-shirt, and my tennis shoes, I left the house.

The drive to Collin's was mercifully short and I was soon pulling up in front of his house. The moving truck was still in the driveway, and it looked like the movers were loading the last of the boxes. Taking a deep breath, I stepped out of my car and went to the front door.

Collin met me on the front steps, wrapping me in his arms.

"Good morning, baby."

"It may be morning, but it's not a very good one," I mumbled into his chest.

Pulling back from me, he looked deep into my eyes. His fingers brushed back a few strands of hair from my face that had come loose from their binding.

"I know."

I buried my head against his chest again and just stood there in his arms, never wanting to leave.

"Come on, let's get inside."

Keeping his arm around my waist, he guided me into the mostly empty house. Lacey was sitting on the family room floor with crayons and a coloring book. Spying me as we entered, she jumped up and ran toward us. I caught her in my arms, picked her up, and hugged her tightly. She was such a darling little girl, and I had grown to love her. Lacey had been through moves so many times before that this seemed normal to her.

"Hey, Lacey."

I tried to be cheerful for her, knowing that it was still hard for her to grasp the concept of distance and how things would change after they moved. She had mentioned several times about having play dates with Riley. The two kids had said their goodbyes at the park yesterday, both unaware that it would be a long time before they would see each other again, if at all. To them, yesterday was just like any other day.

"Hi, Bailey. You're going to visit us all the time, right?"

Looking into her sweet face, so full of innocence, made my heart catch. "I'll try, I promise."

Seeming to accept that answer, Lacey ran back to her coloring, somewhat oblivious to all the commotion around her. Collin pulled me up to his room where he was finishing the last of his packing. Entering his bare room was difficult: all of his furniture was gone, and only a couple of boxes remained in the center of the room with a pile of clothes sitting next to them. I sat down cross-legged in front of the clothes, folding and placing them in the box nearest to me. Collin sat down next to me, our arms brushing slightly. Sitting on the floor was difficult for him with his cast still in place, but he managed.

"Bailey, you don't have to fold those."

"I need to do something, Collin. I can't just sit here, I'll go crazy."

"Okay."

We sat there in silence as we finished up the pile of clothes and taped the boxes shut, labeling them with a black marker. It was pure agony for me knowing that our time was quickly running out. When we were done, Collin pulled himself up and then reached his hand down to help me up.

"I'll carry these last boxes downstairs, then let's go sit out on the porch swing for a bit, okay?"

"Okay." Grabbing the smaller box, I followed behind.

Jared was downstairs when we entered the family room.

"Hi, Bailey, good to see you again. Thanks for helping us over the past couple of weeks."

"You're welcome."

I tried to smile. I knew he wasn't just being polite and that he was genuinely grateful, but helping them pack was the very last thing I wanted to be doing. Instead I just wanted to yell at him, Why? Why are you taking away the best thing in my life?! Keeping my thoughts to myself, I followed Collin out the door and cuddled up on the swing next to him. His arm wrapped around my shoulder, and I leaned against his side.

"I don't think I'll be able to get back this weekend, but I promise I'll come the following weekend."

"Okay."

"I'll get the computer hooked up right away so we can talk on it through the web cam."

I nodded in agreement; words were too difficult for me right now. Every second I felt like I was going to burst into tears and never stop. Not being able to see him every day was going to be one of the hardest things for me. We both had installed programs on our computers so that we could see each other through the monitors, but it wouldn't be the same.

The minutes slipped into hours, and before long, it was lunchtime. The moving truck had already departed, and the last items were being loaded in the cars. Jared had ordered pizza, and the four of us sat on the porch eating. Lacey chatted away, but I only caught a few things she was saying. Collin was watching me intently, concern evident in his eyes. Trying to force down the pizza wasn't working; it seemed to get caught in my throat. Pieces that did make it to my stomach felt like they were going to come right back up. I swallowed soda in a feeble attempt to keep my stomach settled. Too quickly, lunch was finished, and I helped pick up, throwing away my half-eaten slice of pizza.

The agony of goodbyes was approaching, and I hoped I would be able to get through them. Lacey had gathered her doll and blankets and packed them in the car. The house had been cleaned up, and a last walk-through revealed everything had been removed. Doors were locked, and everyone gathered at the cars.

Jared walked over to me; he began to reach out his hand to shake mine, but then seemed to change his mind and instead leaned over and hugged me.

"You are a very special young lady, Bailey. I'm glad my kids got to know you. You will always be welcome in our house, anytime."

"Thanks, Jared."

Lacey was next, and I scooped her up in my arms and kissed her on the forehead.

"You be a good girl, okay? And take care of Collin for me. I'll come see you as soon as I can. I love you."

"Okay, and you'll bring Riley too?"

"Umm...we'll have to see." I pasted on a smile as I looked down into her eager face.

Jared stepped up then and took Lacey to the car to buckle her in.

"Collin, I'll drive around the corner to give you guys some privacy."

"Thanks, Dad."

Collin's hand found mine and we walked slowly to his new car that was sitting in the driveway. He'd been able to find another Camaro, so close in appearance to the one that was totaled. This one was a year newer, but still needed some work. We were at the driver's side; I leaned my back against the door, Collin in front of me. His arms wound around my waist pulling me closer, his eyes piercing mine with such intensity I thought my body would burst into flames. His right hand reached up to my left cheek, holding my face gently.

"I love you, more than I ever thought possible. I will always be here for you."

I wanted to say something like, "Well, you won't actually be *here* for me," but I knew it was childish. My eyes filled with the tears I could no longer hold back, and they poured down my face. "I love you too, Collin. I don't know what I'm going to do without you here."

"This is only temporary, baby. I promise. I will come see you as often as I can. Nothing can keep me from you now that I've found you."

Looking deep into the blue depths of his eyes, I could see he was starting to lose his composure. His eyes were filling with tears, too; when a few slipped down his cheeks, it was my complete undoing.

"Oh, Collin."

Sobbing, I buried my head in his chest. My arms wrapped around his back pulling him as tightly to me as I could, clinging to him for dear life. He rested his chin on top of my head, his arms wrapped around me, embracing me just as tightly. Then, kissing the top of my head, he slowly pulled me back, his hands holding my face just inches from his.

My hands reached up to gently wipe the tears from his face, the emotion between us so strong. We were connected in a way I never thought was possible. His lips captured mine, the kiss full of love and pain. Gently, and then more intensely, it was not like our other kisses; it was full of sorrow and goodbyes. Neither of us wanted to stop, but eventually, Collin broke the kiss, backing away slightly. Still close enough that our foreheads touched, his nose rubbed slightly against mine, his fingers brushing aside the tears from my face.

"I love you, my sweet Bailey. I'll see you soon."

"I love you too, so much it hurts. Please drive safe."

"I will. I'll call you when I get to Vegas, okay?"

"Okay."

I leaned into him for one last hug and one last kiss. He turned me so that he could slip into his car. I stood alone as he started the car and slowly backed up. Stopping as he reached the end of the driveway, he waved. Waving back, the tears continued to stream from my face. I knew the next year was going to be one of the hardest. Standing there I watched his car until it turned the corner and was out of my sight. Unaware of how long I stood there staring down the street crying, I finally yanked myself out of the haze, went to my car, and numbly drove back home.

Reaching the house, I went straight to my room, not wanting to run into anyone. I threw myself on the unmade bed, curled up, and cried. Still wallowing in my pain and oblivious to the sounds in the house, I was unaware that Mia and Natasha had entered my room until they were sitting down on my bed. When I realized they were there and finally pushed myself up to a seated position on the bed, Mia leaned over and hugged me. I was lucky to have such great friends and knew they would help me get through this somehow.

~ Collin ~

Driving along the endless highway with nothing but desert in my view, my thoughts ran over the events of the morning. My chest was still aching from the pain as my heart was ripped apart watching Bailey throughout the morning. I could see through her pretense, trying so hard to be strong. Her eyes gave away her real feelings, so easy to read. I knew how deeply she was hurting. This move wasn't going to be easy for either of us.

Bailey had come crashing into my life so unexpectedly. She had somehow completely taken over every aspect. It was hard to remember what life had been like without her in it. Every minute I was separated from her was going to be agony.

The morning had slipped by much too quickly, and as I had stood there with Bailey in my arms saying goodbye, I didn't know if I could actually drive away. The love I felt for her ran deep, making me feel out of control, as if I was no longer in charge of my own destiny.

I worried about her; I knew she wasn't sleeping well at night again. The shadows under her eyes were a testimony to that fact, even though she denied it every time I asked her.

When at last I finally had to back my car down the driveway, it took everything I had to leave her. Seeing her standing there alone, tears streaking down her face, and knowing that I was leaving the girl I loved more than anything else in this world was one of the most difficult things I'd ever done in my entire life.

CHAPTER THIRTEEN

~ Bailey ~

Summer was almost over, marked by weekends spent with Collin. My senior year of high school was only a few short weeks away. Collin had kept his promise and drove from Las Vegas almost every weekend, unless he had to work. We had spent hours on the computer and on the phone together. It wasn't quite the same, but it helped ease the pain of not having him close by.

Sleep had escaped me since Collin's graduation, and the dark shadows had reappeared under my eyes. The nightmares, twisted now, had returned, and they were even worse than before. The thought of food made my stomach turn; I was losing weight and my clothes hung on me. I knew Collin was concerned since he commented on it almost every time we were together; the worry was evident on his face.

The time we spent together was always so short. There were the excitement and happiness when he would first arrive and then the agony as he left. The roller coaster of emotions was wearing on me physically. Knowing that I needed to accept and move forward was easy to say, but actually accomplishing it was a completely different story.

I focused instead on my upcoming surprise trip to see Collin. Natasha had an aunt who lived in Las Vegas, so we were planning a visit in the middle of the week. Convincing my aunt and uncle to let us drive up there had taken some time, but they'd reluctantly agreed. It was difficult for me to keep my excitement down every time I talked with Collin, but I didn't want to spoil the surprise. I'd already packed my suitcase for the trip and anxiously waited for the next few days to crawl by.

~ *Savannah* ~

It was a Wednesday morning at the end of August. Already the temperatures were soaring outside. In Las Vegas it was unbearably hot even in the middle of the night. I had enjoyed spending most of the last couple of months at Collin's house. This morning I was curled up on the couch sitting next to Collin while we watched a movie. Glancing at Collin's profile I was pleased that my relationship with Collin was progressing. Though wishing things would move quicker, I was at least satisfied that I was making headway. Since the McKenna family's arrival in Las Vegas, I had been careful to play the friendship role only, spending a lot of time at their house helping with Lacey. I explained to Collin how I would always be there for him as a friend if he needed someone to lean on. I had treasured the years of friendship that we'd had over the years, and I didn't want to ruin that.

The first few weeks, he had been reluctant and cautious, but before long, he started to relax and let down his guard around me. We had spent a lot of time together just hanging out like we had when we were little, and I knew that I was slowly winning his trust. Collin spent a lot of time talking about Bailey and how special she was to him. Hearing how much he loved Bailey made me sick, but I would smile instead and not let my anger show.

As summer slipped away, I noticed a change in Collin. The constant separation from Bailey and the long drives were starting to affect him. Collin began confiding to me how worried he was about Bailey. He had mentioned that she wasn't sleeping well and that he was afraid he was jeopardizing her health. I felt like the time was right, so I began carefully planting seeds of doubt in Collin's head about continuing his relationship with Bailey. I was always aware that I had to angle the comments toward helping Bailey. I had learned on several occasions that any negative comment about Bailey would send Collin into complete defensive mode.

Focusing back on the movie I was watching with Collin, I was content for now that I was the one spending time with Collin at the moment and not Bailey. My arm brushed up against Collin's, but I was careful not to seem overly friendly. Pulling my leg up underneath me, I relaxed on the sofa.

"Collin, I need some help." Lacey wandered into the room, standing with her arms behind her.

"Sure. Savannah, I'll be right back." Collin stood up from the sofa and followed Lacey out of the room.

I hit the pause button on the remote and waited for Collin to return. As I waited for him, I realized he had left his cell phone on the coffee table and that it was signaling a text message. Unable to resist, I quickly glanced around to make sure I was alone and then picked it up. The message was from his friend Quinn.

hey, wanted to give u a heads up that Natasha and Bailey are headed to see u. supposed to be a surprise, but wanted to make sure u were home when they got there, they should be there around 2

Rage boiled inside me. Things were going too smoothly right now! I didn't want Bailey here; she would cause a major setback for me. Almost as fast as the anger surfaced, an idea popped in my head.

thanks! I'll be here. talk to u later

Immediately deleting both texts, I settled back on the sofa to wait for Collin to return. Mentally crossing my fingers, I hoped that my quickly formulated plan would work. Now to just set the pieces in place.

"Sorry about that, what did I miss?" Collin asked as he came back into the living room.

"Nothing. I paused it for you."

"Cool, thanks."

Reaching the couch, Collin sat down on the opposite side; much to my dismay, he left a significant distance between us. Sighing, I picked up the remote and handed it to Collin for him to restart the movie.

The movie came to an end, the credits rolling over the screen when Collin flipped off the DVD player. Crossing the family room to the DVD player, he pulled out the DVD and placed it back in its holder.

"Hey, are you hungry?" I asked him.

"Yeah, a little bit. I need to get lunch ready for Lacey."

"Were you going to return the movie today?"

"Probably, why? Did you want to take it for Ashley?"

"No, I think she's already seen it. I was thinking we could grab some pizza. We could take Lacey, or I could stay here with her while you pick it up."

"Sure, I can just pick it up. Lacey loves pizza, and I know she isn't going to want to leave right now."

"I can call it in for you."

"That would be great. I'll run up and tell Lacey."

Picking up the phone, I called in the order. My heart was starting to beat faster. I hoped this worked; maybe things were starting to turn in my favor. As I hung up the phone, Collin came into the kitchen. "Lacey is upstairs playing. I'll be back in a little bit."

"Okay."

Collin grabbed his keys off the counter and left the kitchen. The clock on the microwave read one forty-five p.m.

~ *Bailey* ~

The desolate miles were slowly clicking away. The speedometer on my car was set at seventy-five miles per hour. I wished I could go faster, but I knew pushing my luck would not be a good idea. If I got a speeding ticket, my aunt and uncle would never let me drive to

Las Vegas again. Natasha sat in the passenger seat chatting, about what exactly I wasn't sure. The music from the radio in the background was crackling in and out as reception faded. Leaning over, I flipped on the CD that was loaded and focused back on the endless road in front of me.

Nearing the Nevada state line, a flat dry riverbed appeared with the first casinos just small dots on the horizon. We were in the home stretch now. Miles and miles of sandy dirt spread out from the highway, spotted with cactus, Joshua trees, and prickly shrubs. Heat waves radiated above the surface of the highway, the gauge on the mirror reading that the outside temperature was 111°.

My anticipation was growing; I could barely contain the excitement. Natasha held our directions on her lap. I knew we still had over an hour before we would hit the outskirts of Vegas, and I hoped it would go by quickly.

I tried to focus on what Natasha was saying, but my mind was—where else? With Collin. The days had dragged on without Collin. There were times I wondered how I was going to make it through the next year. Having Savannah so close to Collin also worried me. I knew she had been spending a lot of time at his house. Collin didn't talk much about her, knowing it made me upset and worried. The wondering, though, was almost worse, not knowing if he was really telling me everything. My mind was sometimes my own worst enemy. Imagining Savannah with her hands on Collin, kissing him was a nightmare that had taken over my waking hours as well.

There had been a couple of times that I had been talking to Collin on the computer with the web cam when Savannah had popped into the room and I could see her in the background. Whenever Savannah came up, Collin always played down the subject. Wanting desperately to believe that there was nothing going on, I would try to ignore her, but each time it chipped a piece of my heart.

Looking out over the barren landscape, I wondered why anyone would choose to live out in this harsh land. As I glanced at the odometer, I realized we were now only about thirty minutes away. My heart started beating faster. I resisted the urge to press harder on the gas pedal and kept the car at a reasonable pace.

The highway twisted through low mountains, and as we came around the last bend, the city of Las Vegas stretched out in front of us. Natasha unfolded her directions and we started looking for our exit.

"We'll stop at Collin's first. I know you are dying to see him."

Grinning at my friend, I replied, "Thanks, the suspense is killing me."

"I know. I can see it all over your face. I'm glad you finally were able to talk your aunt and uncle into letting us drive out here."

"Yeah, no kidding. Maybe after this trip, they might let us do it more often."

"That would be cool."

The vast landscape was now becoming more populated. Houses, apartment buildings, and other buildings were multiplying as we drove along the highway. The numerous casinos shaped the skyline in the distance. It was an awesome sight to see. Traffic was increasing, and it was amazing to me how quickly the scenery had changed.

"Okay, it looks like our exit is coming up here. We're going to go to the left when we get off."

At our exit, I guided my car off the freeway and down the off-ramp. Taking the overpass, we followed the road as it wound through the surrounding neighborhoods. I marveled at how similar the houses looked to Riverview, but with sand and rock yards instead of grass.

"All right, it should be four houses down on the right."

"Okay." The blood pumping through my body had quickened with excitement. Finally, the two-story house appeared and I pulled up to the curb. I didn't see Collin's car in the driveway, and my heart began to sink. Natasha seemed to read my thoughts.

"The car could be in the garage."

"You're right. Let's go find out."

"Worst case, they aren't home, and we can come back after a while. Maybe he just ran an errand or something."

We both got out of the car, the oppressive heat pounding us. Walking up the sidewalk, we reached the front door of the dark brown stucco house. Sweat was already forming on my forehead and trickling down my back. With my breath held, I pushed the doorbell and waited. Standing at the front door with Natasha at my left I pushed the button again. Still nothing. Disappointment hit me full force. After driving several hours, the letdown of Collin not being at home was huge.

"Well, I guess no one is home. We'll go to your aunt's house and come back later."

"Just a little longer. You'll see him soon."

We had turned and were walking back down when I heard the door latch click. I spun around, heart pounding. The door opened wider and just inside the dark house stood a blonde beauty: Savannah. My heart felt like it had been ripped out in one instant. What was she doing here?

"Wow, Bailey, I certainly didn't expect to see you. You're a long way from home. What are you doing here?"

Pulling myself together, I tried to keep my voice steady and not betray the anger and hurt that were quickly overwhelming me.

"I could ask the same thing of you. Why are you here?"

"Collin and I are hanging out like usual. We just finished a movie and he went to pick up lunch. I would have gone with him, but Lacey was playing so I stayed with her."

All my fears and insecurities hit me. They were seeing each other, and Collin just didn't know how to tell me. I felt my world starting to spin completely out of control. I could feel Natasha beside me, her hand now resting on my waist. My mouth was suddenly dry, and I was having difficulty forming words.

"I see. So how long has this been going on?"

"Awhile now. Hasn't Collin said anything to you?"

"No, just that you guys were friends."

"We are friends. Good friends. He's confided in me a lot about you. How worried he is about your health. I have to say you aren't looking very well, Bailey.

Are you sleeping at night? The bags under your eyes aren't very flattering."

I felt as if the wind had been knocked out of me. What had Collin told her? A sense of betrayal washed over me. Was he just stringing me along, uncertain of how to deal with me? He had confided in her that he was worried about my health? I thought I was going to throw up. I choked down the bile that had risen to my throat. It was then that I realized Natasha was speaking.

"That's enough, Savannah. Don't play your games with us. I can see right through you. You just couldn't wait to get your hands on Collin, could you?" The anger in her voice pierced through each word.

"Natasha, I have no idea what you are talking about. Collin and I have known each other for years before Bailey even met him. I already had my hands on him." Smiling, she seemed completely confident standing there in Collin's doorway.

I gazed into Savannah's brown eyes and saw nothing but coldness. I had clearly underestimated her. I was beginning to wonder now if she'd had a hand in Collin's family moving to Vegas. Before I could reply to her, I heard the rumble of a car rounding the corner, so similar to Collin's old car I was sure it was him. Looking over my shoulder, I watched the burgundy Camaro come into sight and pull into the driveway. My eyes made direct contact with Collin's through the windshield; the electric current raced through my body. I could see the amazement on his face. I had clearly surprised him.

Collin opened his door and exited his car, a pizza box in his hands. The blue T-shirt he was wearing brought out the sparkle in his eyes, and his presence just took my breath away.

"Bailey? What are you doing here?"

The anger and hurt still pulsed through me.

"I thought I'd surprise you with a visit. But I can see you're not missing me much. Savannah seems to be keeping you company."

For a second, confusion clouded his usually clear eyes and then he turned toward Savannah at the door. Quickly taking the last few steps toward her, he handed the pizza box over to her.

"Savannah, please take this inside and let Lacey know lunch is here. I need to talk to Bailey."

"Sure, babe, no problem." Savannah took the pizza box and disappeared into the house calling for Lacey. I watched her perfect silhouette vanishing down the hall. Before I could force my eyes back to Collin, he leaned over and shut the door. The endearment Savannah had just used was still ringing in my ears. Natasha was still at my side giving me much-needed strength.

"This is a surprise. I had no idea you were coming for a visit."

"That's obvious. I thought you would be excited to see me, but it sure doesn't look like that."

"I'm just shocked."

"What is going on here? Is what Savannah says true? Are you guys hanging out, watching movies and stuff together?"

"Yes."

Just yes? That's it, no other explanation? The knife twisted deeper in my heart. I had hoped he would deny it. My emotions were completely overwhelming me. Trying to focus was becoming difficult.

"Did you tell her about my nightmares? That you are worried about my health?"

"I talk about you a lot."

"Uh-huh. More like how you don't know how to get rid of me? Poor, fragile Bailey—I can hear it now."

"Bailey, you are a very special girl. You deserve so much more."

"Why? Why did you keep coming to see me? Why drag this on?"

"I wanted to make sure you were okay."

"That's it? You wanted to make sure I was okay?"

"Yes."

"So is this it? Where do we stand, Collin?"

"The distance is hard on you. You can't deny that you aren't sleeping well; it's taking a toll on you physically. Maybe it's better to take some time apart."

The words stunned me. I looked into Collin's deep blue eyes, and I felt like I was staring at a stranger. I couldn't believe it. Really, I had been expecting him to deny everything, to take me into his arms, to hold me and make all my fears and pain go away. Instead he stood there just a couple of feet away, unmoving, his face emotionless. I was completely numb.

"Fine. If that's what you want. Go back to your precious Savannah. Let me tell you, Collin McKenna. I have survived worse. I don't need your pity. Your pretty little Savannah, I knew it was always her that you wanted. I was just a charity case for you. Did it make you feel better about yourself by helping the poor broken girl?"

The bitterness that washed over me caused the words to come flying out without any thought to what I was saying. I wasn't thinking clearly enough to stop the fling of insults. In the end, it didn't make me feel any better. My blood was still boiling as it pumped through my veins. I wanted to strike back, to inflict the same pain that I was feeling. But it only left me even emptier inside; and now on top of the pain, I felt regret, wanting to do things over, to say something different. The need to throw something was overwhelming. I wanted to shout and scream at the top of my lungs. Instead I stood in shock. It was finally Natasha tugging on me that snapped me out of my haze long enough to move my feet down the sidewalk.

"Bailey, come on, let's go." Natasha started dragging me toward the car, but then we stopped abruptly and I felt Natasha turn around.

"I thought you were one of the good guys, Collin, but I guess I was wrong. You're even worse because you played the caring, sensitive guy. You and Savannah deserve each other because her conniving little black heart suits you."

Natasha turned and kept dragging me away from Collin. I let her pry the keys out of my hand as she opened the passenger door for me and walked around to get in the driver's side. Mechanically, I slid into the seat. As we drove away from the house, I glanced back to look at Collin one last time and found Savannah standing by Collin's side, her arm resting on his. The horrific image burned into my brain and I couldn't get it out. Nausea overwhelmed me—I thought I was going to need Natasha to pull the car over.

I was completely unaware of my surroundings. The grayness had completely overtaken me. I didn't even know we had stopped at another house. Looking up I realized it must be Natasha's aunt's house. I was in no mood to stay in this horrible city. I just wanted to get home as fast as possible and get far away from Collin.

"Please, please Tasha, can we just go home?" I pleaded with her.

"Stay here and just give me a minute, okay?"

I just nodded and sat in the car, the engine still running, the air conditioning blowing my hair and drying the tears that streamed silently from my eyes.

~ *Collin* ~

The smell of pizza wafted through the car. I was anxiously waiting for the next few days to pass so that I could see Bailey. Being separated from her was more difficult than I'd ever imagined. As I turned down my street there was a car in front of my house and it looked like Bailey's car. No, it couldn't be, I was just imagining things. Then as I got closer and drove into the driveway, I knew it was Bailey, and Natasha was with her. How? Why was she here? My heart pounded with the thrill of seeing her.

As I shut off the car, I caught her gaze, and instantly, pain shot through me. Her eyes weren't filled with love and excitement; they were full of anger and hurt. I was baffled: Why was she so upset? Racking my brain, I tried to think of something that I might have done to hurt her, but I was drawing a blank. She had seemed fine last night when I had talked to her, and even this morning when I had texted her everything seemed to be okay. This sudden change worried me even more.

The dark shadows under her eyes were worse than they were just a week ago; the smudges seemed to grow gradually darker every time I saw her. I knew she had been losing some weight too, but she was so thin now, her clothes were beginning to hang on her. I knew it was my fault. Getting out of my car with a heavy heart, I knew what I must do. I had to let her go, give her a chance to heal. Holding on to her like this was only hurting her worse.

Standing firm, I let her angry words wash over me. She had every right to be hurt and upset. She had needed me and I had deserted her. She deserved better, and I hoped that someday she'd forgive me. Every muscle in my body ached to pull her close, to hold her, keep her next to me, never letting go. Instead I held back, trying not to waiver in my decision.

Our gazes connected, I saw the moment the realization hit her, and as the light in her eyes dulled, I almost lost my resolve. Her pain cut through me so deeply I wondered if I'd ever be the same again. Watching her walk away from me, I felt like half of myself was being ripped apart. As she reached the end of the sidewalk, my thoughts screamed words that only I could hear. *"I'm so sorry, Bailey. And I'm sorry that I always seem to be sorry. I will always love you."*

I watched in silence as the love of my life drove away. I wondered if I'd ever see her again. I knew I needed to give her some space, as hard as it was. I was so focused on Bailey that I was surprised when I turned and Savannah was standing by my side with her hand on my arm. I wondered how long she had been standing there, as I never heard her come through the door.

CHAPTER FOURTEEN

~ Bailey ~

$\mathcal{M}$y senior year was in full swing, and I moved from day to day, going through the motions, but not really living. Halloween had arrived, the weather still warm during the day but cooling at night. It had been over two months since that fateful trip to Las Vegas. The first few weeks had been the worst, with my friends constantly dragging me out of the house trying to cheer me up. My aunt and uncle had been supportive, but they didn't really know what to do with me. I tried to keep up a good front, not wanting to worry everyone, but I knew my aunt could see right through the facade.

Deep down, I knew that it had been too good to last. I was not one of the lucky ones who got to live a fairy tale life. I knew that firsthand, but I had let myself believe and hope that maybe, just maybe, things could be right for me. I realized now that love is not just excitement, tenderness, feeling special; it is also a bone-crushing reality of pain. It felt as if my heart had been ripped entirely out of my body, but the paradox was, the heartache was the only thing that felt real right now.

Maybe the potential for agony and loss is what

makes love itself that much stronger, knowing that it all can be gone in an instant, so you live life like there may not be a tomorrow. Collin would always hold a special place in my heart, no matter how much I tried to forget him or push him out. He had left his mark on me, and it was something I would never be able to remove. I was glad we hadn't taken things any further sexually. I knew if we had things would be even worse. Waiting had been the right decision.

So many times I had composed e-mails and text messages to him but always ended up deleting them or saving them, never sending them. Collin had sent one text message on our drive home from Las Vegas, just two little words:

I'm sorry

I wasn't sure which was worse, keeping that message stored in my phone or the other message that I had saved from before my trip:

love u babe! u r the best thing in my life

Mia had found them both in my phone one day and begged me to delete them, saying I needed to move on and forget about Collin, but every time I tried to delete them, I just couldn't. I wasn't ready yet.

Riley had been my salvation, my special little man. He was so easy to love, so loving in return, his sweet nature helped to ease the pain in my heart. Tonight I was taking him trick-or-treating and was anxious to see what his costume would be. It was a secret he had actually kept from me, no matter how many times I tried to get him to tell me.

Arriving at the Howard house just before sunset, I noticed that the jack-o-lantern that Riley and I had carved the day before was at the front door, its goofy grin glowing with a candle. The lopsided grin made me smile. Riley had worked so hard trying to carve it straight. I actually thought it looked better crooked as it gave the pumpkin more personality. Before I could ring the doorbell, the door flew open.

"Surprise!" Riley yelled.

"You're a pirate!" On Riley's head sat a black felt hat with a skull on the front, and he had a big gold hoop earring hooked to one ear, a black eye patch, white shirt, black vest with a bright red sash tied around his waist, black pants, and black boots. A sword in one hand completed the look. He was entirely too cute.

"I'm three now, a big boy pirate to protect you."

My heart melted instantly, and I thought I was going to cry. I leaned down to hug him. "Yes, you are a big boy now. You can protect me anytime. Are you ready to go trick-or-treating? See what kind of candy you can get?"

"Yes!"

"Okay, let's go get your pumpkin basket."

When I got up, my eyes caught Eileen's, and I could see compassion in them. Eileen had been easy to talk to after I got back from Las Vegas. I was able to open up to her more than my aunt or friends; she had been a sympathetic listener, never judging, and had given me some good advice. I knew that the torture she had gone through in losing her husband, Tucker, was entirely worse than the suffering I was living through right now, and she had survived. She had made it through, and I knew in time I would pull through as well.

"I'm ready! Got my pumpkin!"

"Well, then, let's get going. We'll be back in a bit."

"Have fun!, I'll stay here and man the door."

Eileen walked us to the front door and outside. Dusk was settling over the neighborhood and small children with parents in tow were beginning to flood the sidewalks. Ghosts, princesses, scary monsters, cartoon characters were all out seeking candy and excitement. Eileen waved as we walked to the neighbor's house. Riley animatedly chattered nonstop as we progressed through the neighborhood. Several streets later and with a near overflowing pumpkin, my little pirate was starting to tire out.

"My feet hurt. I'm tired."

"Okay, little guy, let's head back. I think you've got plenty of candy."

I took the heavy pumpkin from Riley, and we started walking slowly back to the house. A few streets from the house Riley abruptly stopped, pulling me to a halt beside him, his big brown eyes staring up at me.

"Baiwey, carry me. Pwease?"

Chuckling, I agreed. There was no way I could resist his plea and sweet little face.

"Let's go."

I reached down and picked him up, carrying him the rest of the way home. His arms wrapped around my neck, his head nestled against my shoulder. The love I felt for this little boy was overwhelming, and I knew I was blessed that he was a part of my life. Though it didn't erase the pain from losing Collin, it did help ease it.

Reaching the house, we went inside to sort through the goods. Pouring out the pumpkin on the table Riley proceeded to sort the candy by type, creating lines of all the different candies. It amazed me how his little brain worked, always organizing and sorting things.

Riley's bedtime was approaching, and I stayed to help Eileen get him ready for bed. Upstairs he played in the bath with his boats and bubbles. After drying him off and getting his pajamas on, I snuggled with him on his toddler bed and read his favorite stories. Leaning over I kissed his forehead.

"'Night, Riley."

Riley reached up and put his hands on my cheeks. "Baiwey, you love me!" Not a question, just a completely honest statement.

"Yes, Riley, I love you!" I never failed to be surprised by what came out of his mouth, but it always made me smile. I wished that he would always be so honest and up front with his feelings as he grew older, but knew that the innocence would vanish as the years passed. I was glad I had the chance to enjoy him now.

Getting up from the low bed, I turned on his lullaby music, shut the light off, and quietly left his room. Downstairs Eileen was in the kitchen putting away dishes.

"Riley's in bed."

"Thanks, Bailey, I really appreciate the help."

"You've got a very special little boy there. Do you know what he said to me when I was tucking him in?"

"No, what?"

"He said 'Bailey, you love me.' Not I love you, Bailey, or asking me if I loved him—just a straight fact, point blank. To top it off, he said it after putting both hands on my cheeks to make sure he had my full attention."

Eileen started laughing. "That's Riley for you. I fear I'm going to have my hands full as he gets older."

"No doubt! He's already a heartbreaker."

I climbed up on one of the kitchen stools at the bar counter as Eileen finished putting away the last few dishes.

"Yes, he is. How are you doing, by the way?"

"I'm okay, I guess. It is getting a little easier, like you said it would."

"I'm sorry things had to turn out like they did. I really liked Collin. I really believe that things happen for reasons. While we're going through it, we don't know why, but somewhere down the road we'll understand. Each experience in life teaches us something; it helps us grow and be a better person."

"I know. Collin was the first person that helped me accept that I shouldn't feel guilty that I survived the accident when the rest of my family didn't. He also pointed out that if the accident hadn't happened, I wouldn't be living here and would never have met you or Riley. That maybe there was a force pulling me here. That maybe you and Riley needed me."

Eileen turned from the sink, tears glistening in her eyes. "We did need you. You have been so important to me and so good for Riley. I have often thought the same thing. Losing Tucker was horrible, and I never want to go through such agony again, but that event brought me back here as well. I believe that you and

Collin are meant to be as well. There is a connection and bond between you that is rare. So don't lose all hope —you just never know what might happen down the road."

"I'm not holding my breath. Lacey and Savannah are his life right now, he made that perfectly clear. It's hard though; so many little things make me think of him. I miss him so much."

"It's only natural that you miss him. I miss Tucker every day. You've become a stronger person, though. Maybe you don't see it or feel it, but I can see it in you. You blossomed with Collin in your life, but you still held on to your fears, like you couldn't shake them. Recently, you are more confident, more self-assured. You do deserve to find happiness in your life, and it will happen."

"I know. You're right. I've been sleeping a little better the last few nights, and it is easier to think of Collin without bursting into tears. It's bittersweet, though."

"I understand. It's still difficult for me to go through photo albums. To roll over at night and not have Tucker by my side is hard. He often teased me unmercifully and I would get so angry, but now what I wouldn't give for him to tease me. I long for him to leave the toilet seat up, or to squish the toothpaste from the center instead of rolling it up the bottom. Those little things that bugged me so badly then are now precious memories. I realize that getting upset over such trivial things was such a waste. It's the little quirky things that I think about so much, and it's all those little things that I can't get back. To look at Riley and see so much of his father in him, and know that he'll never have the chance to know his dad, is really hard."

"I can't even imagine how you have survived."

"I had to for Riley's sake. There were times I just wanted to crawl in my bed, yank the covers up over me, and never come out. I would grab one of Tucker's old shirts that I hadn't washed, where I could still smell his cologne, and hug it tightly against me and cry until the tears wouldn't come anymore. So many of those times Riley would come creeping in, like he knew I needed him. He'd hug me, and I knew that I was lucky. I still had a piece of Tucker with me in Riley.

"I would always hold the memories of Tucker in my heart, and no one could ever take those away from me. So I continued to get up and moved forward. One day leads to the next, and before long, you realize that weeks have passed and you're still moving forward, and then months have slipped by. The pain starts to lighten, and you realize that life does go on."

I slipped off the bar stool and walked the few steps to where Eileen stood and gave her a big hug.

"Thanks. I can't tell you how much your help and support have meant to me."

Eileen's arms wrapped around me tightly, and then she stepped back. "Thank you, Bailey. It goes both ways. I'm so sorry you've had to experience so much heartache in your short life, but things will get better."

"I'll survive, right?" I attempted a slight smile.

Eileen reached over and squeezed me one last time.

She smiled at me. "Yes, you will, and in the end you'll be stronger."

A HEALING HEART

~ *Collin* ~

It was another day at work. I glanced over at the clock for the hundredth time and wasn't surprised that it had barely moved from the last time I'd looked at it. The days dragged on without Bailey. So many times I had picked up my phone to call her but then stopped myself. I knew that I had to leave her alone. I couldn't be the cause of any more pain for her; she'd been through too much as it was. She was strong, and I knew she'd get through this and eventually find someone else to love, someone who could give her more than I could. But she would always hold a special place in my heart, and I doubted anyone else would ever be able to claim it like she had.

Thanksgiving was almost here, and this year I wasn't looking forward to the holidays. Over the past few months, I had kept in contact with Quinn. I tried to be as casual as possible asking questions about Bailey and finding out how she was doing. So far, Quinn had said that she wasn't dating anyone, and on the one hand, that at least comforted me somewhat. But on the other hand, I wouldn't blame her if she was seeing someone else. After all, I was the one that pushed her away; I wanted her to be happy and move on.

Lacey asked about Bailey often, always wondering when Bailey was going to be coming to see her again and wanting a play date with Riley. It was hard to find answers that Lacey would accept. I had tried to explain the truth to her, but she seemed to conveniently misunderstand and not accept what I told her. I guess that was the privilege of being five: you could create your own world. I couldn't blame her. Life could be cruel, and she would learn that soon enough, so there was no need to push the issue with her now. Maybe I'd at least be able to find a way to arrange for her to see Riley again.

Over the past few months, Savannah had been a constant companion. I knew she wanted more than friendship from me. I had been very blunt with her, letting her know I wasn't looking for anything more than friendship. She seemed to have accepted that and we had found a comfortable truce between us, so now I was able to enjoy her company. I cared about Savannah. I probably always would in some fashion; she had been a part of my life for too long.

The more time I spent with Savannah though the more I realized the connection that Bailey and I had was unique. The energy that would pulse through me whenever we had been together was like nothing I had ever felt before with a girl.

Trying to focus back on the line of customers I had in front of me, I caught the smell of Bailey's perfume in the air. My heart started pounding, and I quickly glanced around, searching the faces in the store for any glimpse of the love of my life. Could she really be here? It was then I realized that it wasn't Bailey; it was a girl in her early twenties who was next in line. When she stepped forward to put her items on the counter, the fragrance of her perfume was almost overwhelmingly intense. My heart fell, and I chided myself; did I really expect Bailey to be here? No, I knew better. I smiled at the lady and proceeded to ring up her items. I was really beginning to question my sanity though and wondered if I would ever get over Bailey. Turning back to my register, I finished helping those in my line.

Finally, much to my relief, my shift was over. After clocking out, I left the store and walked outside. The sun was setting in the distance and the weather was starting to turn cold. For all the extreme heat in the summer, Las Vegas could get pretty cold during the winter. As I was sliding into the Camaro's driver's seat, a text from Quinn came through.

> **Bailey's in the hospital. They think it's her appendix, she's going into surgery. Just thought u might want to know**

It was as if the life and air had been sucked from me. She had to be okay. People had their appendixes removed all the time, but this was Bailey and the thought of her going into surgery sent a stab of fear through my stomach.

> **Collin: is she ok? what happened?**
> **Quinn: Natasha and Bailey had gone to lunch yesterday. She was home sick today, thought it was food poisoning. Pains got worse, her aunt took her to the Dr. & they ended up in the ER**
> **Collin: keep me posted, when's surgery?**
> **Quinn: they r prepping her now**
> **Collin: ok, thanks**
> **Quinn: no problem, I'll let u know when I hear anything else**
> **Collin: ok**

The pain in my chest increased. I knew she'd be all right; but I ached to be there to make sure with my own eyes that she was okay. Starting my car, I left the parking lot and drove home, my thoughts flying in a million different directions. Before I reached home, I had made my mind up. I knew that I had to go see Bailey, to make sure she was okay, that I wouldn't be able to rest without seeing her myself.

After reaching the house, I ran up the stairs, taking them two at a time. Finding an overnight bag buried in my closet, I began throwing items in. I called my manager and asked for the next couple of days off; luckily it had been slow, and they would be able to cover my shifts. Grabbing my bag off the bed, I went downstairs to let dad know where I was going and was on the road in less than thirty minutes.

~ *Bailey* ~

Lying in the hospital bed, I felt like my stomach was on fire and that a thousand knives were being shoved into it. My aunt sat at my side holding my hand. I hated the hospital, and being in here brought back too many bad memories. I curled into a ball, but nothing helped. The pain radiated everywhere; it was almost as bad as my broken ribs had been.

"It's going to be okay. Just a little while longer. You're going to be fine," my aunt tried to soothe me.

"It hurts, bad."

"I know, honey. They're getting everything ready."

"Just make it go away," I pleaded.

The nurse came in then and shot a sedative in my IV. Almost immediately I felt calmer, and so sleepy. The last thing I remembered was my aunt kissing my forehead.

A HEALING HEART

I was groggy and my side hurt, but thankfully, not like it had before. I could hear the moan escape my lips as I shifted in the bed. There was a scent swirling in the room that was vaguely familiar, but I couldn't place it. Just when I thought I could focus on it, the memory would slip away. I tried to open my eyes, but everything was blurry. There was a dark shape standing in the corner of the room, just next to the door. I tried to focus on it. It seemed familiar and a nagging sensation rolled through my body. It almost looked like Collin. Then I knew I wasn't awake yet, I must be dreaming, 'cause there was no way Collin could be here in my room. His name was on my tongue, I called out, but when I turned to focus on the shadow, it was gone. I slipped back into the darkness and slept without dreams.

The sun was streaming in my room, the brightness tugging me out of my deep sleep. I felt queasy, and it took me a minute to orient myself before I remembered I was in a hospital room. Opening my eyes, I found my aunt in a chair across the room asleep. Her head was kinked to the side; I feared she would have a stiff neck when she woke up. They had moved me into a different room; this one was smaller than the one I had been in previously. The smell of flowers was overpowering, and I noticed on the counter near the sink there were already several vases full of them and some balloons. The slight noise of me trying to sit up in bed woke my aunt. She immediately jumped up and came over to my side.

"You're awake. Good. How are you feeling?"

"Sore, but better."

"You gave us quite a scare. They said everything went well—your appendix hadn't burst yet, so that was good."

"Guess I should be thankful it wasn't worse. Sure felt pretty horrible though."

"Oh, Bailey, you've been through so much. I wish it was me in here and not you."

"It's okay, Aunt Rachelle. I'm just teasing. I'll be okay."

My aunt scooted the chair next to the side of the bed and held my hand. It made me remember when I had sat in a similar chair months ago holding Collin's hand. With that memory another one swam at the edge of my consciousness.

"Hey, is Collin here?"

"No, why?"

"Nothing. Never mind."

"Why, Bailey? Were you expecting him to be here?"

"No, not really. It's just I have this vague impression that he was in my room when I was waking up. But I was probably just dreaming."

"Sorry, honey. I wish I could tell you he was here. I haven't seen him or heard anything from him."

"It's okay. Probably better that way."

"Mia and Natasha are waiting to see you. I'll go let them know you are awake, then you need to rest so that we can get you home."

"Thanks." I closed my eyes and tried to focus on the vague memory—was it real or was it just a dream? I didn't know; I wanted it to be real, longed for Collin to be there, but I knew it was just wishful thinking. Mia and Natasha entered the room then, pulling me from my daydream.

"All right, you scared us to death. I've had enough of hospitals."

"Come on, Mia, be nice. You know Bailey didn't end up in here on purpose," Natasha laughed.

"Oh, yeah, this is exactly how I wanted to spend my Thanksgiving holiday," I joked back.

"How bad does it hurt?" Mia asked.

"It's better now than it was for sure. The pain was intense. But I guess the drugs they gave me were pretty good. I dreamt that Collin was here." I saw the looks that Mia and Natasha gave each other.

"Oh, Bailey, I'm sorry."

"It's okay, Natasha. It's getting easier, I promise. Look, I can actually say his name without dissolving in tears."

Mia came over and gave me a hug. "You're going to be fine. You have us to keep you busy."

"I know; you guys have been great. I don't know what I would have done without you both. You're the best friends anyone could ever ask for."

"I think we should have a big party when we get you out of here," Natasha suggested.

"How about a big slumber party, with popcorn, scary movies, and lots of ice cream?" I asked.

"Absolutely!" Mia agreed.

"Cool. Now to get out of this place. Trust me, you can't get me out of here fast enough!"

~ *Collin* ~

Standing in the corner of the hospital room, I stayed in the shadows. I had been able to slip past Bailey's family and friends in the waiting room so that no one knew I was here. I had gotten lucky and the nurse on duty had been the same one that had taken care of me when I was in here after the car accident. She had remembered me and had allowed me in to Bailey's room.

Seeing Bailey there in the hospital bed was one of the worst things I had to witness. Watching her quietly in the dark, her even breathing, I longed to go over and kiss her, hold her. When she moaned in her drug-induced sleep, the life was sucked out of me. As her eyes fluttered open, my heart raced. Longing to be at her side, my body almost betrayed me. I knew, though, that I needed to slip out of the room before she knew I was there and before anyone else saw me.

As I stepped to the door, Bailey called my name. Hearing her voice, shaky and faint, was almost my complete undoing, stopping me completely in my tracks. I spun around to look back at the hospital bed, but her eyes were closed again. With one last glance, I quietly left the room and walked down the hall to the exit.

CHAPTER FIFTEEN

~ Bailey ~

Christmas break had arrived, and I was enjoying the time off from school. My cousins Darcy and Tanner were home for the holidays, and it was great having them around again. I hadn't realized how much I had missed their company until they were back in the house. My aunt and uncle were excited to have their kids home as well, and there were several family activities planned during our vacation.

Darcy and I stayed up many nights talking about the latest things in our lives. We had been keeping in contact after she had gone to college in Washington the previous fall, but it was different having her back home. She had gotten an internship through her college and had spent the previous summer working. At first I had been a little upset that she wasn't planning on being home during the summer. I had missed her constant smile and our late night chats. But then after everything had happened with Collin, I was glad she wasn't there to witness the heartbreak that I went through. She had lived through enough of my nightmares those two years after the accident.

Darcy was studying English literature; she planned to go on to get her master's degree and teach in a university someday. Talking about college life with her had me realizing that I was going to have to decide soon what I wanted to do next year. Graduation would be here before I knew it, and I needed to focus on my future.

Tanner, had finally been able to get a small vacation from the software company he worked for in the Silicone Valley. He was part of a research and development team and worked long hours so he didn't get home much. My aunt and uncle had been able to visit him on several occasions, but I hadn't seen him for over a year. He'd always been protective of me, and it felt good knowing he was there to turn to if I needed him.

When he had gotten home, we'd had a late night talking while I spilled my guts to him, telling him all about my relationship with Collin. He had been a good shoulder to lean on and told me that life always had unexpected twists and turns and sometimes miracles did happen and maybe things would work out between Collin and me. It was a nice thought, but realistically, I didn't think there was a chance for that.

My aunt was bursting at the seams with excitement as she catered to all three of us and had gone all out this year with decorations. The Christmas tree was up, and the house was full of aromas from baking cookies and other sweets. Presents were slowly gathering at the base of the tree, and every day felt more and more like Christmas. Anticipation was growing in the house, everyone wondering what was in the colorfully wrapped boxes. This time of year was always one of my favorites: I treasured the excitement of finding the perfect gifts for those I loved and watching them open them. Receiving presents was far less interesting to me than giving them.

It was just two days before Christmas, and today I was babysitting Riley. Since the weather was still unseasonably warm, I had promised him I would take him to the park. I had finished getting dressed and was flipping through my jewelry box for a pair of earrings when I came across the necklace from Collin. I stared at it for a long time before I slowly drew it from the back corner where I had tossed it after returning from Las Vegas. I had not been able to look at it or wear it since that last day I had seen Collin. Today, I held the small heart in my hand, the emeralds and diamonds glistening in the light, and I knew I could wear it again.

I realized that the heart with its fragmented parts within a complete heart meant more than just an intriguing design. For so long I had felt that Collin had been the one to heal me, to help me recover from the nightmares that had plagued me. What I didn't understand before was that no one could heal me; I needed to be able to heal myself.

What Collin had given me was the chance to see that I was worthy of surviving, that there was a purpose for me. It was something that he couldn't give me, no matter how much he had told me or shown me—it was something that I had to find within myself and accept.

With the necklace in my hand I tried to focus on remembering what the emerald and diamond represented. The memory was just out of my reach; I couldn't quite grasp it. Sitting on my bed, I clasped the necklace on, the gold chain and pendant cool on my neck. Opening the drawer in my nightstand, I pulled out my journal and flipped back to my birthday and the entry I had written that night.

> ...The emerald representing spring or starting over...that wearing an emerald brings wisdom, and patience, a symbol of love...The diamond a reflection of everlasting love.

It was as if the pendant had been made for me, symbolizing so much more than just a little heart. Suddenly, I knew that even if Collin and I never saw each other again, he had been meant to come into my life, that through his love and the heartbreak of losing him, I learned more about myself than I ever thought possible. I would never be able to thank him enough, though one day I promised myself that I would thank him in person. I didn't harbor any more anger, it had vanished over the months; I only wished him happiness.

Feeling as if a burden had been lifted from my shoulders, I left the house with a sense of peace that I hadn't felt in a long time. I picked up my phone and scrolled through until I found Collin's last text and I finally replied.

Collin, I hope things are good. I wanted to say thank you. I realize now what you'd been trying to show me. I needed to stand on my own two feet. You will always hold a special place in my heart, and I'll never forget you.

~ *Collin* ~

Savannah was waiting for me downstairs. I'd promised to take her to a Christmas party one of her friends was having. I wasn't thrilled to be going, but didn't really have anything else going on so I told her I'd take her. I had already warned her that I wasn't planning on staying long.

I went to grab my cell phone from my dresser and realized I must have left it downstairs. I entered the kitchen and noticed Savannah—her back to me—had my phone in her hand looking through it. *What the heck?* I thought to myself.

"Savannah? What are you doing?"

I knew I'd startled her as she jumped when I said her name. She turned and quickly smiled; I could see she was trying to hide my phone in her hand.

"Nothing, just waiting for you. You look great by the way. Are you ready?"

"What are you doing with my phone?"

"What do you mean?"

"My phone, can I have it back?"

"Oh, yeah, sorry. I thought I'd pick it up for you so you didn't forget it."

"Why are you even looking through it?"

"I wasn't! Why would you say something like that? Here, sorry I was just trying to be helpful."

She held it out and I took it, realizing I needed to change my passcode. It was then I noticed that my text messages to Bailey were open and there was a new one that she'd just sent. I hadn't heard from her since that fateful day during the summer. I quickly read it, a nagging sensation ran through me as I watched Savannah shift nervously.

"Why are you reading my text messages?"

"Come on Collin, why would I do that?"

Her voice cracked just slightly. If I didn't know her better I might have missed the slight inflection.

"I don't know. That's why I'm asking." My voice had gotten deeper and was edged with anger. I was tired of the games. "Savannah, I'm not playing here, you better answer me and be honest."

"Okay, fine. Your phone went off, and I was curious. I didn't mean anything by it."

"How many other times have you messed with my phone?"

"I haven't. Honest."

I was angry now, I could tell she was lying. How had I been so blind? I let the years of our past friendship get in the way of what was so blatantly obvious now.

"I'm so done with the lying. Savannah. I can see straight through you. I'm going to ask one more time, and if our friendship means anything you'd better answer truthfully. How many times have you messed with my phone?" My voice was on the verge of yelling. I reined it in as a deadly calm washed over me.

"I haven't."

I watched her face closely and noticed that she couldn't keep eye contact with me. Thinking back I realized there was something off that day Bailey surprised me by showing up in Vegas. And the day during spring break when my phone had strangely not charged even when I knew I'd plugged it in. I couldn't prove that Savannah had touched my phone, but all the evidence pointed that way. She was the common denominator.

"Whatever. I have no idea what's happened to you over the past couple of years, but you are *not* the girl I grew up with. I knew something wasn't right, but I just couldn't pinpoint it. I trusted you as a friend, but all you are is a conniving liar."

"Collin!" She screeched as she stepped to me grasping my arm. "I'm not lying. I promise. I haven't done anything. Why are you being like this?"

I shook her off me; her touch made me sick. "Like what? Finally seeing through your crap?"

"Okay, fine, yes I may have touched your phone before but it was nothing. Collin, come on. I'm sorry."

"When Savannah? When did you touch my phone before?"

"I don't remember; it wasn't anything important."

"Spring break? What about when Bailey showed up here? Or wait, let's really get to the bottom of all of this . . . my dad had never talked about moving to Las Vegas until you showed up. Did you have something to do with that too?"

"Come on, Collin, what does it matter?"

"It matters Savannah. It matters a lot. What are you trying to pull here? I've already told you we're friends; it'll never be more than that."

"Why? Why can't it be more than that? Come on, Collin; we have fun together, we grew up together."

"Because I've never felt like that about you, and I never will. And right now I don't even want to have you as a friend. If you really were a friend you'd want me to be happy, not try to sabotage my happiness."

"Is this all because of Bailey? She's not the one for you, Collin, she never was. You need someone strong, not someone so weak. She walked away, didn't even try to fight for you."

"What did you say to her that day she was here anyways before I got back?" My hands fisted at my sides as I tried to contain my anger, my blood was boiling. I was seeing firsthand a side of Savannah that Bailey had tried to tell me about, and I'd brushed it off. Dumb, I was so dumb; I should have known something else was going on.

"Nothing, I just told her you went for pizza, and then you were back."

"Somehow I'm finding that hard to believe. I can't believe you've turned so cold-hearted. Bailey never did anything to you."

"Oh no? She did the worst thing possible she tried to take you from me!" she shrieked.

"I'm not a possession, Savannah, and I was never yours. I don't know what world you are living in. But you really need to get your crap together. I'm so done with all of this. I don't need it. I don't need your so-called friendship."

"Collin, you don't mean that."

"Oh I do, trust me."

Tears fell from her eyes and I felt nothing. I knew it was just another act. I couldn't stand to even look at her anymore. "Stay away from me and stay away from Lacey. Now please get out of my house."

"Collin! I'm sorry, please."

"No, I'm serious; Savannah—please leave." I turned and walked to the front door, opening it and stood beside it as I waited for her to follow.

"I can't believe you'd throw our friendship away like this." She cried as she walked through the door.

"This wasn't my doing; it was yours. Goodbye, Savannah." I shut the door, locked it, and knew I needed to make things right with Bailey.

~ *Savannah* ~

I left Collin with tears streaming down my face as I practically ran to my car. *Where had I gone wrong?* I'd never seen Collin in such a rage before. He'd always been so calm, so easygoing.

Everything was blurry as I struggled to get my keys into the ignition. I pulled away from the curb and drove into the Las Vegas night. My thoughts drifted back to all the times I had spent with Collin growing up. The good, happy memories, and I wondered was he right? *Where and when had things changed, shifted?* He didn't even want me near Lacey anymore. Was I really that bad of a person? I really cared about Lacey; she was like a sister to me. The thought of never being able to see her or Collin again ripped through my heart and it hurt.

Collin had said that I wasn't the girl he'd grown up with and I wondered where had she gone and could I find her again? Was there any way to mend things?

~ *Bailey* ~

The park was full of people and kids. Riley was running up and down the play equipment—swings and rings and slides—always so full of energy it made me exhausted just watching him. I was sitting on the same bench as I had the day I had encountered Collin here the first time. Today was the first time I could remember without the heart-stopping pain. My hand silently held the necklace at my throat, and it made me smile. The next thing I knew someone had thrown their hands over my eyes, blocking my view.

"Guess who?"

Laughing, because I would know her voice anywhere, I answered, "Darcy."

"Damn, how'd you know?" She removed her hands so I was able to see again. Darcy came around the bench and slid next to me, Tanner close beside her.

"I'm psychic? What are you guys doing here anyway?"

"I thought you just said you're psychic."

"Okay, so I'm only partly psychic," I laughed.

"Tanner and I were out doing last-minute shopping. I knew you would be here with Riley so we just thought we'd stop in and say hi. We got a little something for Riley too. Thought he might like to play with it here at the park."

"Ah, how sweet. I'm sure he'd love that." I was about to call for Riley when he turned and noticed us on the bench and came running. Reaching the bench he threw himself in Darcy's arms. Before she'd gone away to school, Darcy had baby-sat Riley a number of times.

"Darcy! I missed you!"

"Hey, buddy! I've missed you too. Here, this is for you, from Tanner and me."

Darcy presented a big, colorful bag with snowmen all over it and bright red tissue paper sticking out. Riley's face lit up and he was ripping out the tissue paper everywhere. At the bottom of the bag, was a bulldozer truck.

"Yeah! A truck! Can I go play with it?"

"Yes, but what do you say first?" I reminded him.

"Thank you."

"You're welcome. Do you want me to come play with you?" Darcy asked.

"Yes!" Riley reached out his free hand and tugged Darcy with him to the sandbox. Darcy was always a sucker for trucks; she'd been like that since she was little. I laughed as they ran off together. Tanner slid over closer to me.

"She never changes, does she?"

"Nope, I sure hope she has boys when she gets older. If she ends up with girls, they're all going to be tomboys."

I leaned my head on Tanner's shoulder. "It's really good to have you guys home. You shouldn't stay away for so long."

"I know; it's good to be home. You seem to be doing better. I know you've had it kind of rough lately."

"Yeah, well, that's life, right? I'm surviving. I've learned that I am a survivor and that I can get through about anything."

"You are a strong girl. It's just taken you a while to see in yourself what everyone else already knew."

"Yeah, well, I guess I'm just a little slow about some things. Better late than never, right?"

~ *Collin* ~

I stood in the shade of a tree watching Riley play in the sandbox with a pretty girl; she appeared to be a little older than Bailey. I'd never seen her before, but

Riley obviously knew her. Bailey sat on the same bench where she'd been sitting on that first day I had run into her here; strange how things came full circle. This time, however, a guy sat next to her. I was too far away to make out her facial expressions, but I watched as she leaned her head on his shoulder—he was clearly someone that she cared for. My heart sank; it was almost too much to bear.

Ever since the day I had seen Bailey in the hospital, I couldn't get her out of my thoughts. I was always wondering how she was doing, what she was doing; constant thoughts of her overwhelmed me. I'd finally just gotten to the point that I couldn't stand it anymore—I needed to come back and talk to her. I knew it was a possibility that she could be seeing someone, that she had every right to, but I still secretly hoped that she wasn't.

Watching her on the bench next to the guy, she seemed content, happy. As much as I wanted to be the one sitting there beside her, I was glad she had been able to move on. I only wanted her to find happiness—she deserved it—but it also left a huge empty feeling in my heart. Tearing myself away from the scene, I quickly walked back to my car and left the parking lot.

Driving through town, I soon found myself back at the lookout. I parked the car off to the side of the road and sat on the hood, which was still quite warm from the heat of the engine. The valley stretched for miles in the distance. The last time I had been here was after seeing Bailey in the hospital. This was a special place for me, one where I could always find comfort and peace.

The warm wind blew across the hill and with it I caught a faint scent, one that I recognized instantly. I tried to push the memory from my head, knowing it was just my imagination. My mind was just playing tricks on me, but I could swear that I smelled the sweet fragrance of Bailey's perfume.

Closing my eyes, I sat and remembered the first time I had kissed her here under the starlit skies. How perfect and right it had felt. Sighing, I knew I'd better get going; I had a long drive ahead of me. I slid off the hood, standing there for a minute looking over the valley. Her voice stopped me in my tracks.

~ *Bailey* ~

I heard the rumble of a car start, the hair on the back of my neck stood on end. Quickly I sat up and turned around to the parking lot behind me, scanning for the car I hoped to find.

"Hey, are you okay?" Tanner asked.

"Huh?"

"You look like you've seen a ghost."

"Did you hear that?"

"Hear what? What's wrong?"

"Nothing, it just sounded like Collin's car."

"Bailey, Collin's in Las Vegas."

"I know, but it still sounded like his car."

Not seeing the Camaro I was so desperately looking for, I stood up and walked toward the parking lot. Just in the distance, turning the corner was a dark car. I couldn't make out for certain if it was a Camaro or not. My mind started racing—could it be Collin? Or was

I just hearing things? I hurried back to the sandbox where Darcy sat with Riley.

"Darcy, I need a huge favor."

"What? Are you okay? You don't look so good."

"I'm fine. If I go get Riley's car seat, can you take him home in about a half an hour? Eileen should be home then."

"Yeah, why? What's going on?"

"I need to go check something out. I thought I heard and saw Collin's car, and I just need to know if it was him or not."

"If he's gone now, he's long gone."

"Maybe, maybe not. I might know where he is. It's worth a shot. If it wasn't him, then I'm just going for a drive. But I have to know."

"Go! Hurry up!"

I raced to my car, flung the car seat out, ran back to the bench where Tanner still sat, and dropped it at his feet.

"Thanks! See you guys later. Riley, I'll come see you later, okay?

"Okay. Bye, Baiwey."

Grabbing my purse as Tanner held it up for me, I ran back to my car and tore out of the parking lot. My heart was pounding. Was there any possible chance that it was Collin? Could he have come back? Why wouldn't he have stopped to talk to me?

I threaded my way through the streets to the outskirts of town and up the winding streets to the lookout. It was a place I hadn't been able to visit for months, as it held too many painful memories. I hoped that maybe, just maybe, if it had been Collin at the park, he would have come here. As I rounded the last turn, the lookout came into view and my heart leapt. Just ahead, on the side of the road, sat a burgundy Camaro.

Through the back windshield I could see the dark shadow of someone sitting on the hood. Excitement shot through me—it *had* to be him, the shadow so familiar, the same one that haunted my dreams. Parking my car behind the Camaro I got out, as I shut the door, I expected the sound to startle the owner of the shadow, but there wasn't any acknowledgment. I *knew* it was Collin—it had to be. My heart was beating so loudly now, I was sure he could hear it from far away. I walked the last few steps to the boy I would love forever.

I watched him slide off his hood, but he just stood there. "Collin?" I was surprised at how steady my voice was, but so quiet; I wasn't sure he had heard me. Then he turned, his face full of shock.

"Bailey? What are you doing here?"

It felt so good to hear his voice again! Shivers ran down my spine. "Looking for you."

"How'd you know I was here?"

"I didn't. I took a wild guess. I thought I heard your car at the park. Was it you? Were you there?"

"Yes, I was there."

"Why didn't you come talk to me?"

"I didn't want to interrupt you."

"Didn't want to interrupt me from what? I'm confused."

"You were with your new boyfriend."

"My what?" I wasn't following. What new boyfriend? What was he talking about?

"The guy you were sitting next to on the bench, you were leaning on his shoulder."

"You mean Tanner?"

"Is that his name? I'm happy for you, Bailey, really I am. I just wanted to see how you were doing. Make sure you were okay. I think about you a lot."

"Collin, Tanner isn't my boyfriend. He's my cousin."

"He's your what?"

"My cousin, Tanner. He's home for Christmas. You never met him because he lives up in the Silicone Valley. My other cousin, Darcy, was there at the park too, playing with Riley."

"So he's not your boyfriend?"

"No, I'm not seeing anyone right now. Haven't seen anyone since you." I took the last few steps closer to him, standing now just a few feet from him.

"Oh."

"Are you still seeing Savannah?"

"No, I never was."

"What do you mean you never were?"

"Savannah has always just been a friend, Bailey. Nothing more than that ever."

"What about that day in Las Vegas?"

"When I saw you standing there, I was so excited to see you. But then I looked at you, I mean, really looked at you. I could tell that our being so far apart was hurting you. It was like you were withering away, so skinny; I knew you weren't sleeping again. I felt horrible. I knew I was responsible, and I couldn't do it anymore. I thought if I let you go, maybe you would forget about me and be able to move on with your life.

"And Savannah, I'm not sure what happened to her. She's not the same girl I grew up with. I caught her going through my phone. I called her out on it. She tried to shrug it off, but I know her too well, I knew she was lying to me. I got her to partially admit to messing with my phone as well as other things.

"I told her to get out of my house. I never wanted to talk to her again."

He took the last few steps toward me until our faces were just inches apart. Shivers ran through my body; his hand reached up and rested on my cheek.

"Oh, Collin," I sighed, as I leaned into his hand.

"I'm so sorry, Bailey. I just came to see how you were. You're looking good, by the way. I just needed to know that you were happy, that's all I've ever wanted for you, and it looks like you are."

"All I've wanted is you, Collin. I'll admit I was hurt, deeply hurt. There were days I didn't know if I was going to get through the pain. But I realized that no matter what, I would always love you. You gave me back my life, healed my heart in a way no one else could. I want to thank you for that."

His face leaned closer to me, his eyes intense as I looked into them. He leaned slightly to me, his lips touching mine, lightly at first, then more passionately, his other hand cradling the back of my head, pulling me closer to him. My arms instinctively wrapped around his neck, bringing our bodies closer together. I felt like I was home; this was where I belonged. Our hearts melded together as one. Breaking the kiss much too soon for my liking, he kept hold of me, leaning back only far enough to be able to look into my eyes.

"I love you, Bailey Walsh. I always have, I always will."

"Oh, Collin, I love you. I never thought it was possible to love someone so much. I wanted you to come see me so badly. I even thought I saw you in the hospital. I had to have my appendix taken out right before Thanksgiving. I dreamed that you were there with me."

Smiling at me, he said, "I was there. Quinn let me know what had happened. I couldn't stand the thought of you in surgery; I had to know you were okay, to see with my own eyes that you were okay. I left before anyone saw me."

"I knew it! I thought I was crazy, but I felt you, felt your presence in the room. It calmed me."

"You called my name. I thought you had seen me."

"I vaguely remember that. I couldn't be sure, I just saw a dark shadow, but it was more a feeling I had."

"I'm sorry, sorry I just left you. I didn't know what else to do. I didn't want to disrupt your life any more than I already had."

For a few minutes, we were quiet, just cherishing the moment, enjoying the time we had together. But there were questions—I had to be sure.

"So, where do we go from here?"

"I guess we'll have to figure that out as we go along. All I know right now is that I love you and need you in my life."

"And I love you, always and forever."

His hand stroked my cheek and I felt completely whole again. My world had been righted; I had survived and would continue to move forward with Collin by my side. The future was unknown, but it didn't matter. All that mattered was that we were together. Dusk was upon us and as Collin leaned to kiss me again, the first star appeared in the sky.

EPILOGUE

~ *Bailey* ~

The morning of my graduation dawned gloomy with heavy cloud cover. Tossing my blankets off, I wasn't going to let the clouds get me down. My senior year was over, Collin and I had survived our long-distance relationship over the last six months, and I anxiously waited to start the next chapter of my life. After graduation, I would be returning to Las Vegas with Collin to attend college there so that we could be closer to each other. We were taking each day as it came, beginning to make plans for our future.

I pulled out my graduation gown and honor cords, humming as I laid them out. Darcy, still asleep in her bed, woke long enough to throw a pillow at me.

"Go back to bed! It's too early," she grumbled at me.

"Can't. I'm too excited."

I laughed as she rolled over and clutched the covers over her head; she had never been a morning person.

Both Darcy and Tanner had come home for my graduation. Collin was in town, staying with Quinn, and we were all planning to go out to dinner after the ceremony. I moved through the morning, getting ready. Eventually, it was time to leave for the stadium. Collin was picking me up and I waited in the kitchen until he arrived.

The doorbell chimed and I hurried to answer it. Collin stood there, handsome as ever in his dress shirt, tie, and dress pants. In his arms he held two dozen fire and ice roses.

"For the graduate. Graduating with honors, to boot. I'm so proud of you!"

"Thanks, Collin, they are gorgeous." I took the huge bouquet from him as he wrapped me in his arms and kissed me.

"Love you."

"Love you too."

With his arm slung around my waist, we walked back to the kitchen where the rest of my family waited. Looking at my aunt and uncle and cousins beaming with pride, I knew I was loved. Even though my dad, mom, brother, and sister were no longer there to see me graduate in person, I knew they would've been proud of me and happy for me. They were there with me in my heart, where they would always be. I placed my beautiful flowers in a large vase and got ready to leave.

"Wait, I've got one more present for you before we leave."

"I don't need anything else, Collin, really."

"We'll see. Come here." From his pocket he took out a small gold package with a shiny green bow on top.

I knew my eyes had gotten as big as saucers. Taking the package from him hesitantly, I looked intently into the blue depths of his eyes. Every eye in the room was on me. I could hear my aunt's quick intake of breath when I took the package.

"Collin, what have you done?" I asked.

"Just open it."

Slowly I ripped the paper off, revealing a small white leather box. Almost afraid to open it, I looked up at Collin's smiling face.

"Hurry up and open it," Darcy said anxiously next to me.

Carefully I snapped the lid open. Nestled in the white satin was a ring: a thin, yellow gold band, with a small emerald center stone, flanked on each side by three baguette diamonds. It was simple and small, and I loved it.

"Oh, my gosh, Collin, it's beautiful."

"It's a promise ring. I promise to love you forever."

I removed the ring out from its box and Collin slid it onto my left ring finger. Tears of happiness welled up in my eyes.

"And I promise to love you forever and always," I reciprocated. I leaned up; placing my hands on Collin's face, I kissed his lips. "Thank you. Thank you for saving me, for loving me, for coming into my life and turning everything completely upside down—or right side up."

"No, I think it was more like you turning *my* life upside down. I love you."

He chuckled as he held me tightly to his chest. I knew my hair was getting messed up, but I didn't care. I was where I was meant to be, in my own personal heaven.

About the Author:

MELISSA A HANSON lives in Southern California, with her husband and two sons. Growing up in Southern California, inspiration for the city of "Riverview" is based on her hometown. *A Healing Heart* is her first completed novel a book 1 of the Riverview Series.

If you would like to follow Melissa A. Hanson, you can do so through:

Facebook: www.facebook.com/mahwriting
Web: www.mahwriting.com

Coming Summer 2015:

Riverview Series Book 2

Follows Mia Kinney
at the Beginning of her First Year of College.

MELISSA A. HANSON

WWW.MAHWRITING.COM